TOO MUCH IN LOVE

"It was nothing," Bill said. "Dana had tickets to a movie, and she asked me to go with her!"

"Why didn't you tell me?" DeeDee sobbed.

"You've been acting so strange lately," Bill said. "I thought it might upset you."

"Are you going to do anything with Dana again?" DeeDee asked, brushing the angry tears from her eyes.

"I don't know," Bill said defensively. "Since when do I have to ask you for permission to do everything? I just don't know what's gotten into you these days!"

"You don't understand anything!" DeeDee shrieked. The minute the words left her mouth she wished she hadn't said them.

"Maybe I don't," Bill muttered. "I sure as hell don't understand what's gotten into you, Dee. And the way things are going, maybe it's time we called it quits!"

Bantam Books in the Sweet Valley High Series
Ask your bookseller for the books you have missed

SWEET VALLEY HIGH

Too MUCH IN LOVE

Written by
Kate William

Created by
FRANCINE PASCAL

BANTAM BOOKS
TORONTO · NEW YORK · LONDON · SYDNEY · AUCKLAND

RL 6, IL age 12 and up

TOO MUCH IN LOVE
A Bantam Book / September 1985

Sweet Valley High is a trademark of Francine Pascal

Conceived by Francine Pascal

Produced by Cloverdale Press, Inc.

Cover art by James Mathewuse

ISBN 0-553-25133-3

Published simultaneously in the United States and Canada

Bantam Books are published by Bantam Books, Inc. Its trademark, consisting of the
words ''Bantam Books'' and the portrayal of a rooster, is Registered in U.S. Patent
and Trademark Office and in other countries. Marca Registrada. Bantam Books,
Inc., 666 Fifth Avenue, New York, New York 10103.

PRINTED IN THE UNITED STATES OF AMERICA

O   13   12   11   10   9   8   7   6

TOO MUCH IN LOVE

One

"I feel left out," Mr. Wakefield complained, looking affectionately at his twin daughters sitting on either side of him at the dinner table. "One day at the office, and it seems like I've been away for about ten years! Now, what's all this I hear about a talent show?"

"It's true, Daddy," Jessica said. "Mr. Collins asked Liz to take charge of the whole thing! He was really impressed with the way she ran the carnival awhile back, and he thinks she's just right for the job this time, too."

Jessica looked proudly across the table at her twin. It was like looking into a mirror. Elizabeth's oval face, framed with shoulder-length, sun-streaked blond hair, was a perfect reflection of her own, from her sparkling, blue-green eyes to the tiny dimple in her left cheek. The physical resemblance between Jessica and Elizabeth was uncanny. But that was only half the story, as Mrs. Wakefield was fond of saying. True, the

1

twins were often mistaken for each other, and from a distance their own parents couldn't differentiate between them. But "up close, and personal," as Alice Wakefield put it, they were as different as night and day.

Elizabeth was dependable, hardworking, and earnest. A committed staff writer for *The Oracle*, the student newspaper at Sweet Valley High, Elizabeth found herself increasingly involved in school activities. *The Oracle* took up a good deal of time, and Mr. Collins, the English teacher who acted as faculty adviser for the paper, had been so impressed with her hard work and organizational ability that he'd been finding new ways to keep her busy. He had recognized the characteristics that Elizabeth was well-known for among her friends and family members. Bright, hardworking, honest, she was always willing to chip in and lend a hand. "Conscientious"—that was the word Mr. Collins had used when he had asked her to be the student chairman of the talent show that morning.

And Jessica—well, Jessica was Jessica. Never on time if being five minutes late would do as well. She'd die of boredom if she had to be cooped up in the *Oracle* office on a gorgeous afternoon. She'd much rather work on her tan at the beach or shop for clothes at the Valley Mall. "Live for the moment," that was Jessica's philosophy. And if it got her into trouble—and trouble, Mr. Wakefield was fond of grumbling, was

Jessica's middle name—well, she could usually count on Elizabeth to come to her rescue.

Jessica always had a million schemes under way at the same time, and she couldn't help teasing her twin sometimes for being so cautious about everything. But deep down, Jessica adored her sister and would do anything rather than hurt her. She was feeling especially close to Elizabeth right now, thanks to the events of the past few weeks—events that still hurt Jessica when she thought about them.

Jessica had decided that her family didn't love her as much as they loved Elizabeth. She knew now she was crazy to have felt that way, but it was still easy to see how it had happened. Elizabeth was so good at everything she did and never got into trouble, while she herself was always getting into scrapes and causing her family to lose patience with her. One thing had led to another, and finally Jessica had convinced herself that no one loved her at all. Thanks to the influence of a new friend named Nicky Shepard, she'd actually tried to run away from home. Luckily Elizabeth and Steven, the twins' older brother, had caught up with her before she got all the way to San Francisco. Jessica still felt sick when she remembered that bus ride. She had felt so lonely, so cut off from everything she'd ever known. . . .

Anyway, that was all history now, and Jessica was determined never to act like such an idiot again. In fact she could barely imagine how she'd let her self-confidence crumble as it had. Proud as she was of her twin, she was perfectly happy being Jessica Wakefield. In fact, she wouldn't dream of being any other way.

"The talent show sounds like a lot of work," Alice Wakefield said thoughtfully, looking at Elizabeth as she passed her the salad bowl. "Are you sure you're not taking on too much responsibility, honey?"

Jessica giggled. "What about Todd?" she asked slyly. "I bet he's not so happy about this!"

Todd Wilkins was Elizabeth's steady boyfriend. Like the twins, he was a junior at Sweet Valley High. Just thinking about him now—his dark brown eyes, broad shoulders, and lean, athletic build—made Elizabeth's pulse quicken. "Todd doesn't mind," Elizabeth said truthfully. "He's incredibly busy these days himself. He's been working about ten hours a week at his father's office, and with that on top of his sports schedule, he's got almost no time at all!"

"I'll bet you rope him into being in the talent show," Jessica mumbled through a mouthful of salad. "Even if he is too busy."

"Girls," Mrs. Wakfield said, shooting a look across the table at her husband, "your father and I have a serious question for you two."

Jessica sat up straighter, her aqua eyes widening with surprise. It was unusual for her mother to sound so solemn.

"You ask them, Ned," Mrs. Wakefield said,

4

her blue eyes softening. "You're the one who's trained at interrogation!"

Mr. Wakefield was a lawyer, and he was used to being teased by his family about his courtroom manner. He laughed and leaned back in his chair. "Don't look so worried, you two," he told them. "This isn't as serious as all that. In fact, it isn't really serious at all. It has to do with a vacation," he concluded, his dark eyes twinkling.

"A vacation!" Jessica shrieked. "Daddy, are you going to take us to Europe?"

Mr. Wakefield burst out laughing. "Not exactly," he told her. "As a matter of fact, this vacation doesn't include the two of you. That's what we want to talk to you about."

"What do you mean?" Elizabeth asked.

"Well, the case I've been working on is a little more involved than we thought at first," Mr. Wakefield confided. "You may remember my mentioning it to you last week. It involves the illegal importation of goods over the Mexican border. Anyway, to make a long story short, there's a lawyer in Mexico City who has some documents I need. We thought he might be able to come up to Sweet Valley, but he's very busy at his office and can't leave. So it looks like I'm going to have to make the trip down there. And your mother and I decided—"

"I'm about ready for a break myself," Mrs. Wakefield interrupted, her pretty, tanned face relaxing into a smile as she looked from one daughter to the other. "Everything's been such a zoo at the design firm with this Williams project, and I'd be so much better off if I got some rest."

"It's been ages since your mother and I have been away by ourselves," Mr. Wakefield confessed. "And it would be so much nicer for me if she came along. Otherwise, I'm afraid it would be pretty dreary."

"You don't have to explain!" Elizabeth burst out. "For heaven's sake, of course you should go with him, Mom. It sounds like a wonderful trip."

Mrs. Wakefield sighed. "The problem is what to do about the two of you. I thought about asking Mrs. Lawrence over to stay with you, but I wasn't sure—"

"Mother!" Jessica shrieked. "How can you even suggest such a thing? Mrs. Lawrence used to stay with us when we were babies! We don't need a baby-sitter anymore!"

Elizabeth laughed. "*We've* been baby-sitting for other people for years," she pointed out. "You don't have to worry about us! We'll be fine."

"You see, Alice?" Mr. Wakefield said reproachfully. "I told you. They're big girls now!"

"I don't know," Mrs. Wakefield said doubtfully. "After all, it isn't as if we're going to be only an hour or two away. Mexico City is a long way off. And with Steven back at college—if anything were to happen . . ."

The twins' brother Steven had taken some

time off from school, having gone through an especially hard time after the tragic death of his girlfriend, Tricia Martin. Things were beginning to improve, however, and he was back at college again now.

"What," Jessica said pointedly, "could possibly happen?"

"We'll be fine," Elizabeth chimed in. "Honest, Mom. You just go ahead and plan yourself a wonderful vacation. Jessica and I will take care of everything here. We promise!"

"We'll have a wonderful time," Jessica echoed, her blue-green eyes shining. Something wonderful, something far too wonderful to share with her parents or Elizabeth, had just occurred to her. Her parents were going out of town, and she and Elizabeth were going to have the whole house to themselves—entirely, completely, one-hundred percent, and absolutely to themselves!

Elizabeth was upstairs, stretched out on her bed on her stomach, her favorite position for talking on the phone. She had finished the dinner dishes about five minutes earlier, and now she was trying to get in touch with DeeDee Gordon. Mr. Collins had suggested that DeeDee would be a good person to take charge of designing the sets for the talent show, since she was so interested in art. Elizabeth had never hung out with DeeDee, but she had always liked the small, dark-haired girl.

Mrs. Gordon answered the phone, and a minute later DeeDee picked up another extension. She seemed surprised to hear from Elizabeth and listened in silence while Elizabeth explained what Mr. Collins had suggested.

"Me?" DeeDee said at last. "Mr. Collins wants *me* to be in charge of the sets?"

"Why not?" Elizabeth said. "You'd be perfect. Besides, I heard the art teacher say the designs you'd done for the foreign-language festival were *superb*."

"Oh, *those*," DeeDee said disparagingly. "Those were nothing, really. I haven't the faintest idea how I'd go about organizing something as big as this."

"You'd be terrific, DeeDee," Elizabeth said warmly. "I'm sure you have enough experience. Besides, we'll all be helping each other out. It's not going to be a professional show or anything."

DeeDee was quiet for a minute. "I'll have to talk to Bill about it," she said. "Maybe if he's interested in it, then . . ." Her voice trailed off.

Elizabeth sat up on her bed. Bill Chase and DeeDee Gordon had been a couple for some time now. She knew they were very close, but she didn't see what Bill had to do with *this*. Still, she didn't want to interfere. And she really did want DeeDee to help with the show. "When can you let me know?" she asked.

"We-e-e-ll," DeeDee said tentatively, "I'll ask Bill about it as soon as I can. I don't know. I'll try

8

to get back to you tomorrow sometime. How would that be?"

"That's fine," she said politely, although she was confused by DeeDee's hesitation. "We'd really appreciate your help, DeeDee. And thanks for thinking it over."

"What was that all about?" Jessica asked. She had wandered in to hover over her twin, hoping to get Elizabeth off the phone so she could call her friend Lila Fowler. Her news right now was just too good to wait!

Elizabeth shook her head, looking puzzled. "Have you noticed anything strange lately about DeeDee Gordon?" she asked. "Does she seem like she's acting funny all of a sudden?"

Jessica wrinkled her nose. "No stranger than usual," she said. "Why?"

Elizabeth laughed. "I forgot," she said. "You're not exactly objective when it comes to DeeDee, are you?"

"I'm always objective," Jessica said. "Can I help it if DeeDee's a total weirdo?"

Elizabeth's expression was still thoughtful as Jessica flounced out of the room. She wasn't surprised Jessica still felt a little annoyed about DeeDee. It wasn't like her twin to forgive the competition, especially when the competition had won.

Some time ago Jessica had starred in a school play opposite Bill Chase. She had enjoyed flirting with him and making sure he fell head over heels in love with her. But Jessica hadn't taken him seriously until DeeDee got into the picture. DeeDee really cared for Bill. They had a lot in common. They both liked reading, drama, and all kinds of sports, especially surfing.

Once DeeDee got involved, Jessica suddenly couldn't bear the thought of losing Bill. She started to lay it on thick, and Bill almost fell for it.

But Bill had had too much good sense to trade the real thing for a fake. He saw how much DeeDee loved him, and he realized he felt the same way about her. Jessica was edged out of the picture, and Bill and DeeDee had been a twosome ever since.

Still, Elizabeth thought, *that doesn't mean that DeeDee has to consult Bill before signing up for a project!*

She couldn't get over how strange DeeDee had sounded on the phone. She had seemed so insecure, so uncertain. Not like the old DeeDee at all.

I hope everything's OK, Elizabeth thought anxiously.

But a minute later Elizabeth was riffling through a stack of papers on her desk. She had homework to do, a story to revise for *The Oracle*, and six more people to call about the talent show—not to mention Todd, whom she hadn't seen all day!

Worrying about DeeDee Gordon, she decided firmly, was just going to have to wait.

*　*　*

10

"DeeDee!" Mrs. Chase exclaimed, opening the screen door and looking at the girl. "Did Bill know you were coming over tonight? I'm afraid he isn't here!"

"He isn't here?" DeeDee repeated, crestfallen.

"He's at the library, dear," Mrs. Chase explained. "Do you want to come in anyway?" she added, noticing the anxious expression on DeeDee's face. "He had to do some work for history, you see, so he took the car and went over to the library. But was he expecting you?"

DeeDee shook her head. Bill wasn't expecting her, as a matter of fact. But she'd barely seen him all day! She'd tried to call before she came over, but the line had been busy.

DeeDee couldn't believe how disappointed she felt. During the ride over to the Chases' house, she'd been thinking how great it would be to watch television with Bill on the old plaid couch in the basement. They'd make popcorn and just hold each other in the dim light of the television set . . .

"No, thanks," DeeDee said at last when Mrs. Chase urged her again to come inside. "But can you ask Bill to call me as soon as he gets in? I really need to talk to him," she added.

She could hardly blame Bill for going to the library; it wasn't as if he knew she was coming over. But DeeDee couldn't help thinking that a few months before, this sort of thing wouldn't have happened. She and Bill always made plans together then. If he was planning to go to the

11

library, he would have asked her to go along, or said he'd drop by her house afterward.

Something felt wrong to her lately, though she couldn't quite pin it down. They'd had lunch together that day, but Bill had been distant. He didn't seem to be really listening to what she was saying; he had a distracted expression on his face. When she asked him about it, he just said he was worried about his history paper.

And the same thing had happened that day after school. Bill almost always gave her a ride home, but that day he didn't come by her locker as he usually did. She had wandered all over the halls trying to find him. He was talking to Ken Matthews and Roger Patman about something, and she'd had to stand around for ages before he even noticed her.

And then, DeeDee thought miserably, sliding behind the steering wheel, *he barely even talked to me all the way home!*

DeeDee wasn't sure what was bugging Bill, but she had a pretty good idea of what she should do. It was what her mother had once said about her divorce from her father. "We should have just taken more time to spend alone together," her mother had told her grandmother. "We both got too busy, and we ran out of time for each other. And then one thing led to another, and the marriage fell apart."

DeeDee's eyes stung with tears when she remembered the day her father had walked out

12

of the house forever. Watching her parents break up had hurt her terribly.

But that isn't going to happen to Bill and me, she vowed, turning the key in the ignition. *We just need to spend a little more time with each other. And Bill needs to see how much I depend on him, how much I need to be with him. Once he realizes that,* DeeDee thought fiercely, *he won't leave me.*

Not for anything in the world.

Two

"DeeDee," Patty Gilbert complained, shaking her head, "what in the world is wrong with you today? You're barely listening to a word I'm saying."

"Sorry," DeeDee mumbled, pushing her sandwich away and craning her neck to see if Bill had come through the swinging doors to the cafeteria yet. Patty was her best friend, and DeeDee had looked forward to their lunch together all morning. But now she was a million miles away. She couldn't help it. She was worried about Bill. He hadn't called her when he got home the previous night, and he hadn't come by her locker that morning to say hello before homeroom, either.

"I was asking you about your design courses," Patty said impatiently, as if she'd had to repeat her words to get her friend's attention. "How are they going? Is Ms. Jackson as good a teacher as you'd heard she was?"

15

DeeDee stared down at her tray. She'd been too embarrassed to tell Patty that she'd stopped going to the courses at the civic center several weeks before. Somehow they seemed like a waste of time, time she could spend with Bill, DeeDee thought.

Patty Gilbert was a senior, ten months older than DeeDee. A beautiful black girl, with short, dark hair and large, sparkling brown eyes, she was one of the most popular, talented girls in her class. The two girls had met at summer camp when they were little and had been as close as sisters ever since. But DeeDee couldn't help feeling now that theirs was an unequal friendship. Patty was so friendly, so outgoing, while she herself was much quieter, much shyer. For the last couple of weeks, anyway, she had felt less comfortable around her old friend.

"I haven't really been going to the classes anymore," she mumbled, avoiding Patty's gaze. "I've been so busy. . . ."

"But you were looking forward to those classes for ages!" Patty burst out. "You said Ms. Jackson was the best design teacher within a hundred miles!"

"She's OK." DeeDee sighed. "The classes just weren't that helpful, that's all. Not for me, anyway. I just don't think I'm ready yet for that level of training."

Patty looked searchingly at her friend. "You just need confidence. You were recommended to that class by two art teachers, remember?"

16

DeeDee blushed. "I'll pick the classes up again some time. Really, Patty. Don't worry about it." She wished Patty would quit going on about the design courses and get back to their plans for this coming weekend. Patty's boyfriend, Jim Hollis, who lived in a town about two hours' drive away, was coming to Sweet Valley for the weekend, and DeeDee and Bill had made plans to meet them at a Chinese restaurant on Friday night. DeeDee couldn't wait. She really liked Jim, and she had a feeling the evening would help straighten things out between Bill and her. Just being with another couple, seeing how close they were, how much in love . . .

"Are you going to help Liz out with the talent show?" Patty continued, nibbling on a carrot stick. "I ran into her this morning, and she told me she'd asked you to be in charge of the sets. You'd be perfect, Dee, and it would give you more experience."

DeeDee bit her lip. She'd been worrying all day about the talent show, praying she wouldn't run into Elizabeth so she could stall a bit longer. The idea of taking charge of such an important part of the show frightened her. She'd love to try her hand at it, but she was afraid she'd mess the whole thing up. If only she were as confident as Patty!

Besides, there was Bill to think about. If Bill was planning to be in the show, it would be a good way to get to see more of him. He was so incredibly busy these days. Aside from surfing and the special research project he was doing for Mr. Fellows, the history teacher, he was spending about ten hours a week at swim practice. DeeDee felt as if he barely had time for her anymore. And when she did see him, he was tense and distracted.

Just as her father used to be, she thought, remembering his heavy schedule before the divorce. And her mother had only made it worse by filling up every spare minute with her own job and part-time night school.

If I take over the sets for the talent show and Bill isn't involved with it, I may never see him again! DeeDee thought miserably. She wished she could share her fears with Patty. But it didn't seem to be a good idea. After all, Patty saw Jim only once or twice a month. And she never complained.

"I'm not sure yet," DeeDee told Patty. "I'd love to help out, but I have to talk to Bill about it. He may have something in mind for the show already—a skit or something—and he may need my help."

Patty seemed on the verge of saying something but then apparently changed her mind. "I hope you decide to do it," she said at last. "I'm going to be doing a modern-dance routine, and it'll be much more fun if you're involved!"

"Mmm," DeeDee murmured noncommittally. She had just caught sight of Bill coming in through the doors, and she bounced up from her chair, waving at him to come over and join them.

"Thank goodness!" she cried as he made his way through the crowded cafeteria to where she and Patty were sitting. "Bill, I thought you'd disappeared from the face of the earth!"

DeeDee didn't care that Patty was staring at her and shaking her head. DeeDee was too happy to see Bill again to care what *anyone* thought.

Looking anxiously at her watch, DeeDee shifted her weight from one foot to the other. Four-thirty, and still no sign of Bill. *He's usually done with practice by four-fifteen*, she fretted. *What in the world can be keeping him*?

"DeeDee!" an excited voice called. Spinning on her heels, DeeDee saw Bill hurrying out of the locker room, his blond hair combed back after his shower, and a white towel around his neck. "I made it!" he cried, throwing an arm around her neck and giving her a hug. "I qualified for the regionals!"

For a minute DeeDee went blank. Then she remembered that the swim team had been timed that day to see who would qualify for the regional meet. Bill's best stroke was the butterfly, and he'd been practicing for weeks, hoping he'd qualify.

"I'm so glad!" DeeDee said happily, her brown eyes shining under her glossy fringe of bangs. Bill was amazing, she thought. He'd already won every award there was to win in surfing, and he was one of the most talented actors around. He was so good at everything!

I wonder what he sees in you, a nagging little voice inside her whispered. But DeeDee brushed her feeling of inadequacy aside. This was Bill's moment, and she wasn't going to spoil it for him.

"When's the meet?" she asked, slipping her arm through his as they walked together down the hall.

"Friday night," Bill told her. "The day after tomorrow. Can you believe it? I've got so much to do between now and then—and this morning I promised Liz Wakefield that I'd try to do a short reading for the talent show."

DeeDee pulled her arm away and stared reproachfully at Bill. "Friday?" she demanded. "But we've got plans with Patty and Jim Friday night. Don't you remember?"

Bill slapped his hand to his forehead. "Gosh, that's right! I'll have to call Patty and apologize. I'm sure she and Jim will understand. You don't expect me to do anything else, do you?" he asked incredulously, staring at DeeDee as her expression darkened.

"Jim's almost never in town," DeeDee said glumly. "We can't stand them up, Bill. It just isn't fair."

Bill's blue eyes were thoughtful. "Well, then, why don't you go ahead and go out with them?" he suggested, a look of relief appearing on his face. "That way Jim and Patty won't be let down.

20

And maybe we can all meet somewhere later on."

DeeDee felt herself getting frantic. Couldn't Bill see how important it was for them to be together, to be a couple? "I can't go alone!" she exclaimed. "It wouldn't be right."

"Come on, Dee," Bill admonished. "Where's the independent girl I fell in love with? Besides it's only for a couple of hours," he pointed out. "It seems like the most sensible way to handle things."

"Maybe Jim and Patty will come with me to the meet," DeeDee said lamely. "I think that's a much better idea. And then the four of us can go out together later, just like we'd planned."

Bill shrugged. "I don't know," he demurred. "It sounds kind of dumb to me, to be perfectly honest. Why should Jim and Patty want to spend a Friday night at a high-school swim meet, when they could be out somewhere nice? Just go out with them, Dee, and don't turn it into such a big thing."

"But it *is* a big thing!" DeeDee wailed. "It's a weekend night, Bill, and I want to be with you! Is that so strange?"

Bill blinked. "No," he began, "but—"

"I never see you anymore," DeeDee insisted. "You're so busy you don't even have time for me." Tears were welling up in her eyes. "I was really hoping we could have a good time this weekend," she said, a tear sliding down her cheek. "And now . . ."

21

"Dee, I don't know what's gotten into you lately." Bill slipped his arm around her and pulled her tightly against him. "You know how crazy I am about you. And we see each other all the time! We have lunch together, take classes together, study together . . ."

DeeDee drew in a long, quavering breath. "I know," she said at last, trying to sound brave. "I'm sorry, Bill. I think I'm just overly sensitive these days for some reason. I don't know what's gotten into me, either."

"Liz mentioned that you might be taking over the sets for the talent show," Bill remarked, looking at her thoughtfully. "Are you going to do it?"

"Sure," DeeDee said casually, making her mind up then and there and trying not to panic at the prospect of making a complete mess of the whole thing. After all, Bill had said he was going to try to put a dramatic reading together, she reminded herself.

And if things kept going the way they had that week, it looked as if the talent show would be about the only chance she'd have to see Bill!

"I can't believe Mom and Dad are really leaving on Saturday," Jessica said excitedly, turning the rearview mirror toward her so she could check her reflection.

"Cut it out, Jess," Elizabeth said sharply, turning the key in the ignition of the twins' red convertible Fiat. "That mirror's to keep us from getting killed, not for you to admire yourself in!"

"Just think," Jessica said, sighing. She settled back comfortably in the passenger's seat. "Daddy said they'll be gone for at least ten days! We're going to have such a *wonderful* time."

Elizabeth gave her twin a searching look as she backed the Fiat out of the parking space in the Sweet Valley High student lot. "Just what do you mean by 'wonderful time'?" she asked. "You know what Mom and Dad said. We promised them we'd act like responsible adults."

Jessica shook her head wearily. Sometimes her sister's naiveté astounded her. "Do you mean to tell me that you're planning to act the same way you do when they're at home?" she demanded.

Elizabeth laughed. "What's wrong with that?" she asked her sister. "You make it sound like I'm the most boring person on earth!"

"We-ell," Jessica began. "It's not that you're *boring*, Liz. But you have to admit that you don't take many risks."

"Right," Elizabeth said matter-of-factly, slowing down for a red light.

"We've been studying the Brontë sisters in Mr. Collins's class," Jessica added slyly. "And Mr. Collins said they were truly remarkable women because they had vivid imaginations and they took risks all the time."

"Just what have you got in mind?" Elizabeth asked warily. "Are you planning on running through Sweet Valley at midnight screaming 'Heathcliff'?"

"I was thinking," Jessica said, dropping her voice confidentially, "more along the lines of having a party."

"Jessica!" Elizabeth wailed. "We can't have a party if Mom and Dad aren't around! They'll kill us!"

"How would they possibly find out?" Jessica demanded, her blue-green eyes wide with disbelief. "I don't mean a big party," she amended hastily. "Lila and I were just going to invite a few people over. You know, about five or ten. And you and Todd can ask some people, too," she added generously.

Elizabeth groaned. "Leave Todd and me out of it," she suggested. "I think I'm going to have enough of a headache for the next couple of weeks, trying to get this talent show organized. I don't need to drive myself crazy worrying about what disasters might occur once you and Lila have set your friends loose!"

Jessica shook her head, her eyes filled with mock pity. "Poor, poor Liz," she moaned. "Don't you realize you're missing a perfect opportunity to change your whole life and do something wild? It'll be a wonderful party, Liz. Honest. And—"

"Thanks," Elizabeth said firmly, "but no thanks. I think I'm going to leave all the risk-taking to you and Lila this time around. Besides," she added dryly, "something tells me that I'll be able to enjoy the party secondhand. It'll probably be so loud I'll be able to hear it all the way at Todd's house!"

"Don't be silly," Jessica said, shaking her blond hair back from her face. "For goodness sake, Liz, you act like Lila and I are both two-year-olds. Don't you think the two of us have got everything under control?"

Elizabeth shook her head. "I shudder to think," she murmured, turning the Fiat down the shady side street where the Wakefields' attractive, split-level home was located.

Any time Jessica was involved in a plan like this, Elizabeth had learned from experience, there was no point in guessing in advance how things would turn out. There was simply no way to know.

Three

"OK," Elizabeth said loudly, riffling through her papers and looking at the high-spirited group gathered around her in the auditorium of Sweet Valley High. It was Thursday afternoon, and she was trying to compile a final list of the talent-show entrants to give to Mr. Collins. "Patty, you're doing a dance number, right?"

Patty nodded enthusiastically. "It's all set," she assured Elizabeth. "I've got my music picked out and everything."

"Good." Elizabeth smiled. She consulted her list again. "Todd, what are you going to do?" she asked, turning to look into Todd's warm brown eyes.

Winston Egbert, generally known as the clown of the junior class, let out a loud groan. "You two probably have it all planned already," he muttered. "I bet it's something really mushy, like a love scene from *Romeo and Juliet*."

Todd laughed. "Foiled again, Egbert. Actually, I was planning to try my hand at a stand-up comedy routine.''

Elizabeth winked at him, scribbling furiously. "OK, Winston, what are you going to do?" she asked.

"Ken Matthews and I are going to do magic tricks," Winston said solemnly. "And Jessica's going to be our assistant."

"I am?" Jessica asked, looking surprised. "What do I have to do?"

"You'll see," Winston said mysteriously, trying to catch Ken Matthews's eye.

Ken, a well-built, handsome boy, was captain of the football team. His amused gaze rested on Jessica. "Mostly all you have to do is let us cut you in half," he drawled.

"Very funny," Jessica retorted. "If you think I'm going to—"

"OK, OK," Elizabeth broke in, turning to Mr. Collins. "It looks like we've got twelve entries. Each of the acts should be five minutes long, and counting time for set changes and applause and everything, it should run about an hour and a half."

"That's fine," Mr. Collins said, smiling as he looked over Elizabeth's list. "Now, what's going on with the sets? Is DeeDee going to take charge of that?"

"I don't know," Elizabeth admitted, looking troubled. "She said she'd get back to me. I had a feeling that she was going to do it, but she hasn't made a commitment yet."

28

Mr. Collins frowned. "That isn't good," he said softly. "We haven't got much time. We really need a definite answer from her right away."

"I'll be seeing DeeDee later," Patty Gilbert said suddenly. "Should I ask her what's going on, and tell her to get back to you, Liz?"

Elizabeth looked questioningly at Mr. Collins. "I'd really like DeeDee to do it if she can," she began. "But if we're really in a hurry, maybe—"

"No, that sounds like a good idea, Liz," Mr. Collins said quickly. "I'd like DeeDee to help out, too. She's a very talented girl, and I think we'd all benefit if she'd take charge of the sets. So why don't you just let me know what she says."

No wonder Mr. Collins was one of the best-liked teachers at Sweet Valley High, Elizabeth thought, slipping into her denim jacket as the meeting broke up. Jessica thought he was popular because he looked like a movie star. But Elizabeth thought it had more to do with his attitude. Mr. Collins was always willing to be patient, to give his students a break.

"Well, boss," Todd teased, "you really know how to run a meeting. How about a trip to the Dairi Burger?"

"Liz!" an agitated voice called. Elizabeth turned, her eyebrows raised, to face Patty Gilbert. Everyone else had left the auditorium by now, but Patty still looked around her as if to make sure no one was listening.

29

"I'm furious with DeeDee," she burst out. "I'm going to let her have it tonight when I talk to her!"

"Why?" Elizabeth asked, shooting a puzzled look at Todd out of the corner of her eye. Patty and DeeDee were like sisters, she thought. What in the world could DeeDee have done to make Patty mad?

"I said I'd ask her about the sets," Patty said angrily, "but I have a feeling she didn't show up this afternoon because she found out Bill's not going to be in the show."

"What does that have to do with anything?" Elizabeth asked, her confusion growing.

"It's only a hunch." Patty sighed and ran her fingers through her dark curls. "Look," she added, "you two know how crazy I am about Dee. I'm only angry because she's so close to me. She's a terrific friend. But lately . . ."

"Lately what?" Todd probed gently, slipping his arm around Elizabeth.

Patty's brow wrinkled. "Oh, nothing," she said finally. "I just think it's wrong of her not to give you a definite answer," she repeated lamely.

"I still don't understand," Elizabeth said. "As a matter of fact, Bill did ask me this morning if he could cancel the reading he'd planned to do. He's made it to the regionals this weekend, and he's got a special research project he's doing for Mr. Fellows. It sounds like he's swamped. But what does that have to do with DeeDee?"

"It shouldn't have a *thing* to do with her," Patty answered. "But I suspect it does."

"Uh-oh." Elizabeth sighed. "I was kind of worried about this. Do you mean that you think DeeDee won't work on the sets because Bill isn't going to be in the show?"

Patty nodded glumly. "I'll tell you something. A year ago, even a few months ago, DeeDee Gordon was just about the last girl on earth I could imagine saying that about! She's always been one of the most independent people I've ever known. In fact, I used to worry about her. I used to wonder how she'd ever be able to get along with Bill once they started seeing each other all the time. It wasn't that she was headstrong or anything. She just always had her own ideas, her own plans."

"Bill's the same way," Todd said thoughtfully.

"I know." Patty sighed. "Well, DeeDee's changed," she announced, looking from Todd to Elizabeth. "I don't know why, and I'm not even sure I can find out without losing her friendship. All I know is that she won't do anything without Bill anymore. It's like she's his shadow. She doesn't even seem *interested* in anything but Bill! He's all she talks about. She keeps harping on what *he's* doing, the prizes *he's* won. She sounds like a broken record!"

"I can't believe this," Elizabeth said. "DeeDee was never like that!"

"Well, she is now," Patty said bitterly. "I don't know what in the world's gotten into her. It's so

31

frustrating, I can't even tell you. And I don't know how to talk to her about it. How do you tell someone she's started to lose her whole identity?"

"I don't know," Elizabeth said, startled. She and Todd exchanged uneasy glances.

"Still," Patty said, her jaw set, "I'm DeeDee's best friend. And *someone's* got to do something about it!"

"What are you going to do?" Todd asked.

"Well, for one thing, I'm going to make sure DeeDee takes on the sets," Patty said briskly. "She should have let you know right away if she wasn't going to do it. Besides," she added, her brown eyes thoughtful, "I have a feeling that what DeeDee needs most in the world right now is something of her own—something Bill Chase has nothing to do with."

"You know, Patty," Elizabeth said earnestly, "I have a feeling that you may be right."

But would DeeDee be ready to take on the responsibility? she wondered to herself, taking Todd's hand as they walked out of the gym together. That, she had a feeling, might be the hub of the problem.

Meanwhile, on the other side of the school, DeeDee was sitting outside the boys' locker room, doodling absentmindedly in a notebook, waiting for Bill to come out after swim practice. Bill almost tripped over her when he emerged, his hair still wet from the shower and a pile of notes in his hand that he had to give Mr. Fellows before five o'clock.

"Dee!" he cried, startled. "What are you doing here?"

DeeDee clambered to her feet, her face bright red. "Uh—I just thought maybe we could go to the Dairi Burger together or something. I thought you might be hungry."

Bill shook his head. "Didn't I tell you? We're celebrating Mom's birthday tonight. I'm really sorry, Dee, but I've got to run. I promised her I'd be home early, and I've still got to talk to Mr. Fellows about the research project I've been doing for him."

DeeDee bit her lip, tracing the square tiles in the linoleum floor with the toe of her sneaker. "I was really counting on getting to spend a little bit of time with you tonight, Bill. I wanted to ask you about tomorrow night, and—"

"Dee," Bill said, exasperated, "I just don't have time! I promised my mother, and—"

Bill's temple began to throb as he saw DeeDee's lower lip tremble and her brown eyes fill with tears. It was a sight that was all too familiar lately.

He had been in such a good mood a few minutes earlier. His time had been excellent, the best ever, and the swim coach thought he had a good chance of winning the following night. And he'd been looking forward to seeing Mr. Fellows, because the research had turned out to be really fascinating. Bill had volunteered to help Mr. Fellows with the special project because he'd always been interested in the Civil War. The work had proved to be absorbing, and he'd been hoping he and Mr. Fellows could talk about the next stage of the project before he had to race home for dinner.

And now everything was ruined. Bill didn't understand what was going on with DeeDee lately. He felt as if nothing he did was quite enough. If they spent the evening together, she spent almost half the time complaining about how busy he'd been lately or how busy he was *going* to be. It seemed as though he was devoting all the spare time he had to trying to soothe her. And it was beginning to feel like a full-time job.

Bill had known DeeDee for some time before they'd fallen in love. They'd been good friends, in fact. Bill had been helping her with her surfing, and at first, in his infatuation with Jessica Wakefield, he had been blind to DeeDee's special qualities. She was a good friend, that was all.

But before long, Bill began to realize his feelings went much deeper. DeeDee was the warmest, funniest girl he'd ever met. More to the point, she was fun to be with. She was terrific at everything she did—surfing, roller-skating, dancing, all kinds of art. And she was interested in a million things. She loved current events and had told him that she would love to be a politician someday. She was interested in architecture, origami, cooking, dance—even golf! Being with DeeDee was a tremendous relief for Bill. His own interests were varied and demanding. He had been an avid surfer from an early age, and now it looked as though acting was vying for the number-one spot on a very crowded list of extracurricular hobbies.

DeeDee had never demanded that he spend a certain amount of time with her. She didn't believe in restrictions. They saw each other when they liked, and they always had a wonderful time.

Bill wasn't sure when things had started to change, but over the past month or two DeeDee had become increasingly withdrawn. She had actually stopped going to the civic center design classes she'd been so enthusiastic about, and that wasn't like her at all. But when Bill asked her about it, she got defensive.

And when they were together now, it seemed all she wanted to talk about was *him*. In the old days DeeDee loved to argue, and she'd never let him get away with a silly statement. Now, she hung on his every word. It was beginning to make him nervous.

Bill had never felt so confused. He was still in love with DeeDee, but he couldn't bear the pressure she was putting on him. He wanted to see her happy again, involved in things that mattered to her. *Things*, he thought uneasily, *other than me.*

Deep down Bill felt a bit guilty as well. Because

lately he had begun wondering if he and DeeDee really were right for each other after all. His free time—and he had so little of it—was something he treasured. He wanted to have fun again, not feel depressed and sad.

In fact, Dana Larson had cornered him after Spanish class that day and had asked him if he'd go see a movie with her on Saturday afternoon. She knew he was an old-film buff, and she'd gotten two free tickets to the matinee of *My Little Chickadee* from a friend of her father's. Dana was the lead singer for The Droids, Sweet Valley High's rock band, and she looked the part. She was a tall, pretty girl with a short, New Wave haircut, a dynamic smile, and a funky, offbeat wardrobe. Best of all, she was her own person—as independent as could be.

A few weeks before, Bill wouldn't have thought anything of mentioning his plans to DeeDee. But she was acting so strangely these days that he decided he'd just keep quiet about it and save himself a lot of trouble.

"OK," DeeDee was saying now, looking at Bill as if he'd just announced he was planning to move away to Brazil, "I guess I'll just go home then. Did you bring your car today?" she asked hopefully.

Bill sighed heavily, the throb in his temple coming back again. "Yeah," he mumbled, giving up on seeing Mr. Fellows that afternoon. "Let me give you a ride home."

It was pathetic, he thought to himself later,

how grateful DeeDee looked after he suggested that. Like a puppy dog or something, certainly not like the outgoing, vivacious girl he'd fallen in love with a few months earlier.

She was a different person! *It's as if she got body-snatched*, Bill thought. *Somebody came down from outer space and zapped her. They took my DeeDee away and left this strange, sad girl down here in her place.*

And Bill wanted his old DeeDee back. Right away.

Four

"Bill! Bill!" DeeDee yelled, jumping up and down in the bleachers and waving her arms. Patty and Jim exchanged glances. "I don't think he heard me." DeeDee sighed, crestfallen, and settled back down on the hard bench.

"I haven't been to a swim meet in ages," Jim Hollis said affably, looking around him with a mixture of amusement and genuine interest. "Boy, DeeDee, I didn't expect an evening like this when you said the four of us would find a quiet place to talk!"

DeeDee looked crushed. "I couldn't help it," she said defensively. "Bill just found out he made the regionals on Wednesday, and I couldn't very well let him swim knowing no one was here to watch him, could I?"

"I don't know," Jim said, surprised. Patty pressed his hand, and he looked at her in silence for a minute. "Well, how are things going for you this semester?" he asked after a while. "You

39

still keeping up with local politics, or is art winning out these days?"

DeeDee turned back to the pool to avoid Patty's knowing eyes. "I—I haven't been doing much of anything," she mumbled, staring down at the water.

Jim laughed. "That doesn't sound like DeeDee Gordon," he remarked. "Come on and 'fess up. What've you been doing with yourself these days when you're not at swim meets?"

DeeDee chewed nervously on a fingernail. "Not much," she told him. "Really. Hey, it looks like Bill's warming up now!" She leaned forward and craned her neck for a glimpse of the top of Bill's blond head.

Behind her back, Patty rolled her eyes at Jim as if to say, "You see what I mean? I wasn't kidding!"

DeeDee rubbed her hands together nervously, trying to concentrate on the scene before her. The room was very warm and smelled strongly of chlorine, and her nerves felt frazzled from the periodic sound of the gun being fired as the swimmers took off. She hoped Bill won his race. Maybe he'd be in a good mood then, and the four of them could have a nice time afterward.

It seemed strange to her now that she'd actually looked forward to the evening with Patty and Jim. She usually enjoyed Jim's company. But tonight he just kept asking her about what she'd been up to. Patty wasn't behaving like herself, either—not since their phone conversation the night before. Patty had made her feel rotten about the talent show, and she agreed to help out—after she made it clear to Elizabeth that she was going to need a lot of help. Maybe Bill would be willing to chip in, DeeDee had suggested. "He's so wonderful at things like that. . . ."

Elizabeth hadn't said a word.

DeeDee was sick and tired of being asked why she'd given up her art classes at the civic center. Everyone had been bugging her about it—her mother, Patty, Mr. Collins, and now Jim. Even Bill had been upset about it.

But DeeDee had her reasons. They just happened to be reasons she didn't feel like sharing with anyone else.

Not even Bill.

Susan Jackson, the young woman who taught the course, was famous throughout the state for her accomplishments in design. DeeDee had admired her for ages. She'd been so excited about the classes she could hardly contain herself.

And they'd been going well. Ms. Jackson thought DeeDee had a flair for design, and if she kept it up, she could have a profitable career.

Then one afternoon after class Ms. Jackson asked her out for coffee. DeeDee had felt honored to be singled out by the brilliant young teacher. They had had a long talk, and Ms. Jackson had confided a number of things to her star pupil. She told DeeDee, among other things, that she had gotten divorced the previous year.

She said she still didn't feel the same. Sometimes she missed her husband so much she couldn't bear it. But he had already remarried—a quiet, plain young woman with no career. Someone unthreatening, someone who would always be around for him. Not like Susan, whose career had always come first.

Just like my mother, DeeDee had thought forlornly. *She went back to school and got a job, and the next thing I knew my father was walking out the door forever.*

DeeDee was smart enough to put two and two together. She didn't go back to her design classes, and soon after her talk with Ms. Jackson, she began to act differently around Bill.

What matters, she told herself now, *is that he knows I need him. That's what keeps two people together. Before—the way I used to be—I must have made him feel useless, like just another casual friend. But now he knows I depend on him for everything. Nothing else matters but him.*

If Mom had acted like this, DeeDee thought, tears shining in her brown eyes, *maybe Dad wouldn't have left. Maybe—*

But her reverie was interrupted by the announcement that the 100-meter butterfly— Bill's race—was about to begin.

Instantly DeeDee was on her feet, yelling with all her might. Bill looked so handsome as he strolled over to the edge of the pool, shaking his arms to loosen them up! She was so proud of him. She could barely contain herself when the gun went off. The race seemed to take forever: four laps of the twenty-five-meter pool. For the first two laps the swimmer from Lawrence was ahead of Bill by a half-body length, but on the third lap, Bill began to catch up. The two swimmers were neck and neck for most of the last length of the race, but at last Bill pulled ahead, breaking the school record by six-tenths of a second.

DeeDee was beside herself with happiness. Barely aware of what she was doing, she climbed over the feet of the people next to her and raced down the stairs of the bleachers. All she knew was that she wanted Bill to see how proud she was, how much she cared.

A minute later she was pushing through the crowd of swimmers and officials at the foot of the bleachers. Her throat was hoarse from screaming Bill's name.

"Dee! What is it?" Bill demanded, his blue eyes narrowing as she approached, a towel around his shoulders.

It wasn't how she'd imagined the scene at all. Bill didn't look proud to have won, or happy that she was there to watch him, DeeDee thought, recoiling.

He looked embarrassed! He looked as though he wished he didn't even know who she was.

But DeeDee forced herself to approach him, throwing her arms around his neck. "I'm so proud of you," she murmured. "I just had to let you know how proud I am."

She couldn't hear his response. The crowd around them was too noisy. But she could feel his arms stiffen as she tried to pull him closer to her, and she could tell that despite everything she'd done, the evening was ruined.

She was just going to have to try harder from now on.

"I don't know, Lila," Jessica said as the slim, light-brown-haired girl bounced up to turn over the new album she'd bought that afternoon at the mall. "Don't you think thirty people is a few too many? We don't want them to tear down the house or anything."

Lila pushed the lift button on her stereo and plopped herself back down on the cream-colored carpeting in her bedroom. "That's right," she said thoughtfully. "I forgot how *snug* your house is."

Jessica burst out laughing. The Wakefields' house was considered roomy by most people—certainly big enough for the twins, their brother Steven, when he was home from college, and their parents. But the whole house would fit into one wing of the Fowler mansion. Lila's bedroom was almost as big as their whole second floor! "It *is* a shame for the poor people of this world," Jessica said dryly. "But we do what we can, Lila."

Lila either didn't understand Jessica's sarcasm or chose to ignore it. "Now, you know the secret to having a really good party, don't you?" she said, picking up an emery board and filing her long, perfectly shaped nails.

"Tell me," Jessica said, groaning inwardly. True, Lila Fowler was famous for her parties. But Jessica had a feeling that her secret was obvious. There was only one way to get top bands, the latest video equipment, catered food, and elaborate decorations—and that was with money. The Fowlers had tons of money, and Lila felt obliged to do her best to use up what she could of it.

"The secret," Lila said, "is all in the guest list."

"What do you mean?" Jessica asked. For all her teasing, she really *did* want Lila's help. She'd never had a party entirely on her own before. And knowing her parents wouldn't be there made everything seem slightly more risky. Jessica really wanted it to go well.

"Well, take the *men* you invite," Lila said dramatically. "If you just invite the same old stupid guys from school, you might as well be at a dance in the gym or something. Right?" Lila sounded very superior. For the last couple of months she had been dating Drake Howard, a sophomore at Sweet Valley College.

Jessica blinked. Actually she sort of *liked* school dances. But Lila made them sound so unsophisticated, Jessica would rather have died than admitted it.

"You need some older guys like the men in Drake's fraternity. He's in Delta Theta. All the really cute guys are in that one. Anyway, what I suggest you do is let me call Drake and have him bring a few of his friends. You can still ask some guys from school, but this will definitely spice the party up."

"I don't know, Lila," Jessica said. "College guys? Aren't they kind of old? I mean—"

Lila looked at Jessica as if she'd just crawled out of a playpen. "Well, do as you like," she said. "All I can say is that if you ask *me*, a party with the same old childish bunch from school is about as appetizing as—"

"All right, all right," Jessica said. "Call Drake. But just a *few* guys, remember. If my parents—"

"Jessica Wakefield," Lila said, shaking her head in disbelief, "you must think I was born yesterday. Just relax and let me take care of the whole thing. OK?"

"OK," Jessica said faintly, feeling as if she'd just gotten a stomachache. "Only a few of them, right? And—"

"Next Saturday night," Lila said firmly, "at the Wakefields'. Jess, this is going to be the best party to hit Sweet Valley in months!"

"Yeah," Jessica managed. "I'm sure it will be. But—"

"But nothing!" Lila said fiercely. "Now, you just go home and tell your parents *bon voyage*. And you can have dreams all night about your party a week from tomorrow night!"

Or nightmares, Jessica thought uneasily.

But Jessica was too optimistic by nature to let her spirits flag for long. Tomorrow was the day!

Her parents were leaving, and she and Elizabeth would have the house to themselves for days and days and days!

By the time Jessica had gotten home, she felt completely reassured about the plans she and Lila had made for the party.

Lila's right, she told herself. *Having the same old people would be boring.*

And who knows, she thought. *Maybe this time I'll find the man of my dreams: handsome, rich, with a gorgeous car . . .*

Jessica barely even heard her parents' greeting when she went inside the house. She was floating about nine feet off the ground, and nothing—absolutely nothing—was going to bring her down now!

"Todd, what is it?" Elizabeth whispered, looking anxiously into his familiar, coffee-brown eyes and touching his cheek with her hand.

Elizabeth and Todd were parked up at Miller's Point, overlooking the beautiful valley twinkling with lights. As far as Elizabeth was concerned, the evening had been absolutely perfect. They had gone to the swim meet with Enid Rollins, Olivia Davidson, her boyfriend Roger Patman, and a new friend of Enid's, named Paul. Enid was Elizabeth's best friend, and Elizabeth was glad to see her friend enjoying herself on a date, now that she and George Warren were no longer going together. The six of them had gone to the

Dairi Burger afterward for a quick snack and then the couples had gone their separate ways.

But about halfway through the evening, Elizabeth had begun to notice that Todd was being unusually quiet. He didn't eat very much of his hamburger, either, which wasn't like him at all. At first Elizabeth thought she might have said something that rubbed him the wrong way, but when they left the restaurant, he suddenly pulled her close to him, kissing the top of her head. The gesture had been so spontaneous and affectionate that Elizabeth knew that whatever was bothering him, it wasn't her.

Now, at last, they were alone together, and she was able to ask him what was wrong.

"Nothing," Todd said, the expression on his face contradicting his response so sharply that Elizabeth almost smiled.

"Come on," she urged him. "It's me, remember? Liz? Can't you tell me?"

"No," Todd said abruptly. "I can't."

Elizabeth didn't feel like smiling anymore. This sounded serious! "Todd, what is it?"

But Todd refused to tell her what was wrong. "I heard something at the office that's kind of bothering me," he said finally, after she'd urged him to confide in her.

Todd had been working part-time at his father's office for the past few weeks, but Elizabeth couldn't imagine what he might have heard there that would depress him so much.

Nor would he tell her any more. "I really can't," he protested. "Honest, Liz. I would if I could."

"Is it serious?" she asked at last, her curiosity completely unsatisfied.

Todd looked searchingly into her eyes, his expression still clouded. At last he seemed to come to some sort of decision. "No," he whispered, pulling her closer to him. "It isn't serious."

"Well, thank heavens," Elizabeth said, relieved. She laid her head against his chest, listening to the comforting sound of his heartbeat.

"Liz, what would I do without you!" Todd cried suddenly, wrapping his arms around her so tightly she thought she might break in half.

"Goodness!" Elizabeth laughed. "What an insane question!" She smoothed his hair gently with her hand, trying to smooth his agitated spirits with the same gesture.

It's a ridiculous question, she told herself, smiling happily in his arms. *Thank heavens it's one we don't have to consider—even for a single moment.*

Five

It was Saturday morning, and Bill Chase was relishing a few last minutes in bed, watching the square of sunlight dancing on his bedroom wall.

What a week, he thought. This was the first time he'd felt relaxed in ages. The night before . . .

Bill groaned, remembering what a disaster the previous night had been. At first he'd thought everything would go well. The race had been wonderful—he had felt like a million dollars when he realized he'd won.

But then DeeDee had ruined it all by charging down from the bleachers. It was as if he'd won a gold medal in the Olympics, instead of just a race in the high school regionals. He felt so foolish—and he couldn't tell DeeDee he was embarrassed, either. That would have been a giant mistake.

No; Bill realized by now that he couldn't be honest about anything with DeeDee these days. For one thing, she was almost morbidly sensitive. The tiniest little things set her off and made her almost hysterical. It was as if she was looking for trouble between the two of them, Bill mused, his arms behind his neck as he stared thoughtfully up at the ceiling. As if she was so afraid things were going to go wrong that she saw a major disaster brewing all the time.

In Bill's mind, the night before had been the turning point. After the meet he had joined DeeDee, Patty, and Jim, and the four of them had gone to a Chinese restaurant. At first it seemed as if everything would be OK after all. Patty and Jim were both happy to see Bill, and Jim was making them all laugh with his comical attempts to use chopsticks. But about halfway through dinner DeeDee suddenly got very quiet. She excused herself twice to go to the ladies' room, and the second time she was away from the table for such a long time that Patty finally excused herself to go see if anything was wrong.

Later, in the car, DeeDee burst into tears when Bill asked her what the problem had been. "I just felt so stupid all of a sudden," she had mumbled. "You and Patty and Jim all seemed like you were having such a good time, and I felt really left out."

They had already said goodbye to Patty and Jim at the restaurant, and Bill could tell the rest of the evening would be spent trying to reassure DeeDee, insisting that he still loved her, that nothing was wrong. But he just didn't feel like it. He was exhausted; the late hours he'd been keeping suddenly had caught up with him. And he simply couldn't understand the way DeeDee was behaving.

"Look," he had said, more roughly than he'd intended, "you've always said that what matters most between two people is trust. What's happened to that? Don't you trust the way I feel about you? Do you always need to have me spell it out to you?"

DeeDee had just stared at him, her brown eyes shining with tears.

Forget it, Bill said to himself now, sitting up and swinging his legs over the side of the bed. He was supposed to see DeeDee again that night, and he was sure he'd have to go through the whole routine again. For now he fully intended to relax and enjoy the first free Saturday he'd had in ages.

He was supposed to meet Dana at the Plaza Theater at two o'clock, he reminded himself as he stepped into the shower and turned on the hot water, lifting his face into the refreshing spray. He was looking forward to this afternoon. *My Little Chickadee* was one of the few W.C. Fields movies he'd never seen. And Dana was good company—sharp-witted, bright, filled with interesting ideas and plans. Maybe it was being a singer for a rock band that made her so gutsy, Bill reflected. She'd had unusual experiences for a girl her age.

However guilty it made him feel, Bill couldn't help comparing Dana to DeeDee. It wasn't that he was interested in Dana. Not at all. He had learned his lesson about trying to replace one girl with another. *Or,* he thought uneasily, letting the hot water fall on his upturned face, *have* I?

Bill was an only child, and he had never been as outgoing as some of the kids he knew. Maybe that was why he'd spent so much time surfing. It was something he could do entirely on his own. He didn't need other people to help him enjoy it. Spending so much time alone had made him sort of shy, and he hadn't had very much experience with girls before he met the one who changed everything for him—forever.

Her name was Julianne. Bill had sat next to her in math class when he was living in Santa Monica, before his parents were divorced and he and his mother moved to Sweet Valley. Julianne was gorgeous—long blond hair, eyes so blue they sometimes appeared almost purple. At first Bill thought Julianne would never pay any attention to him. He was too shy to talk to her in class. But when they ran into each other while surfing one day, he realized they had a world of things in common. They both loved old movies and Mexican food. They were both only children—and they were both lonely. They needed each other.

He and Julianne had fallen in love. There was only the two of them, and they meant everything to each other. Until that horrible night when they had gotten into a silly argument at a party. . . . Bill could still barely let himself think of that evening without getting choked up.

Julianne had left the party, furious, grabbing a ride home with friends. The driver had just gotten her license. It was raining, and the roads were slippery. Bill had promised himself he'd call Julianne as soon as he got home. He missed her as soon as she left and realized how dumb it was to argue with someone he loved so much.

But Julianne never made it home. Her friend's car slid out of control on a tight curve and exploded against an embankment. Julianne was killed instantly.

Bill had gone through a very bad time after Julianne's death. The night she was killed he was so overcome by grief that he grabbed his surfboard and went into the stormy waters. The tide pulled him out to sea, and he almost drowned. Luckily, a coast guard cutter came to his rescue. Later Bill developed pneumonia. He barely cared whether he lived or died. Julianne was dead, his parents were splitting up, his mother wanted to move, and his whole world seemed to have collapsed around him.

It took a long time, but gradually Bill began to recover. He realized that Julianne would have wanted him to. She would have hated the guilty depression he had been wallowing in; she was so filled with life and love that she would have wanted him to forgive himself for the argument, to go on with his life.

That summer Bill and his mother moved to Sweet Valley, and the change of location helped Bill as he began to rebuild his life. Bit by bit he put the pieces back together—all but one. He couldn't even look at other girls. Julianne was dead, and no one else would do.

And yet, it was the resemblance to Julianne that had made Bill notice Jessica Wakefield at first. The same soft blond hair, the blue-green eyes. . . . He had really fallen for her. It took him a long time to see that Jessica's appearance was the only thing that reminded him of Julianne. Jessica was as fickle as Julianne had been loyal, as manipulative as Julianne had been straightforward. He had seen Jessica solely as a replacement for Julianne, and his infatuation had taught him one thing: Julianne was dead. He would never be able to replace her. If and when he fell in love again, it would have to be because he'd met someone who was special on her own terms.

And that was what had happened with DeeDee. On the surface, no one could have been more different from Julianne. Small, muscular, and less conventionally pretty than the Wakefield twins, DeeDee was appealing because she had such a marvelous personality. Her dark-brown hair, toffee-brown eyes, and sprinkle of freckles looked better and better to Bill as he got to know her. Like Bill, DeeDee had recently suffered the painful rupture of her parents' marriage. She was a sensitive listener, a good friend. She had learned—the hard way—to stand on her own two feet.

But maybe he'd misjudged her, Bill thought now, toweling himself off. Maybe he'd been so eager to fall in love again—after Julianne, after Jessica—that he'd given DeeDee more credit than she'd deserved.

He hoped not.

But the way DeeDee had been acting lately, it was getting harder and harder to tell.

"I just love W.C. Fields," Dana said, reaching into her tub of popcorn and smiling.

"I'm kind of an addict myself," Bill admitted. "I never knew you liked old films, Dana."

"Hitchcock," Dana mumbled, chewing the popcorn and wiping the butter off her fingers with a napkin. "I'm a Hitchcock freak. *Psycho* is my favorite. And *The Birds*—"

Bill looked at Dana with admiration. He'd never met anyone who could sit through *The Birds* without getting petrified.

"But mostly," Dana continued, "I'm a star addict. James Cagney, Katharine Hepburn—I've seen *The Philadelphia Story* at least nine times! I come here all the time," she added, looking around the dim interior of the art-deco-style cinema. "They've got really good film festivals— foreign movies, too. I'm trying to improve my French," she said, giggling, "so I come to all the Truffaut movies and close my eyes. That way I can't see the subtitles."

"How do you find the time to see so many movies?" Bill asked. He knew what a heavy

57

schedule Dana had singing with The Droids. And she was a good student, too.

Dana shrugged. "You know how it is," she said casually. "Sometimes I come here by myself after rehearsing. It's a good way to unwind."

Bill couldn't believe Dana went to the movies by herself. *She's amazing*, he thought admiringly. He wanted to ask her more about her favorite movies, but just then the theater dimmed, and the curtains parted over the big screen. Bill settled back in his seat with anticipation, munching the popcorn Dana offered him. *I have a feeling*, he thought happily, *this is going to be one of the best afternoons I've had in ages.*

"That was excellent!" Dana exclaimed as she and Bill walked out into the bright sunlight. "Even better than I expected."

"Hey," Bill said, blinking as his eyes got used to the sun again, "have you had lunch yet? Maybe we could get something to eat."

"That's a nice idea," Dana said, smiling, "but the guy I'm dating is coming to Sweet Valley this afternoon, and I told him I'd pick him up at the station. Maybe some other time, though. Hey," she added, as if something had just occurred to her. "There's a wonderful rock group that's going to be in from the East Coast next week. And I think The Droids are supposed to get free tickets. So maybe you could come along. They're supposed to be great."

"Sure," Bill said, zipping up his lightweight jacket. "That sounds good. Why don't I give you a call on Monday or Tuesday, or—"

"Bill!" a girl's voice called. "Bill Chase!"

Bill turned around, confused. Suddenly he felt a sinking sensation in his stomach. Jessica Wakefield was waving to him from across the street. She was with Cara Walker, and they were both carrying striped shopping bags.

A minute later Jessica and Cara had darted across the street to join Dana and him on the corner. "What a gorgeous afternoon!" Jessica said slyly, looking at Dana with narrowed eyes. "What have you two been up to? You haven't been wasting a day like this inside a movie theater, have you?"

"Uh—" Bill muttered awkwardly. Of all the rotten luck, he was thinking. Why in the world did they have to run into Jessica and Cara? They'd be sure to tell everyone they'd seen Bill and Dana there together!

"As a matter of fact, we just saw *My Little Chickadee*," Dana said. "But it wasn't a waste of time, was it, Bill?"

"Uh, no," Bill mumbled, his face flaming.

"I'm sure it wasn't," Jessica said, giving Cara a knowing look. "Well, we've got to run, so we'll just leave the two of you here. Nice seeing you, Dana," she called over her shoulder as she started for the red Fiat, parked two cars up from the theater.

59

Damn! Bill thought, jamming his hands in his pockets.

Why did he have to run into someone from school? Especially Jessica, who, he knew, was still angry at him. It just didn't seem fair.

Still, maybe Jessica had better things to do than gossip about him. That was all Bill could hope for, and he wasn't going to let her wreck the nicest afternoon he could remember in weeks. He was just going to forget he'd run into Jessica and Cara. And cross every finger he had that the two of them would do the same.

Because if one of them tells DeeDee, he thought, *it looks like I'm going to be a dead duck.*

Or *Duck Soup,* he thought with a grin, catching a glimpse of the poster for the Marx Brothers movie pasted up on the Plaza billboard.

But he wasn't going to let himself worry about DeeDee. Not yet. He'd had too nice a day so far, and much as he hated to admit it, thinking about DeeDee put a damper on his high spirits.

Six

"I still can't believe we have the whole house to ourselves!" Jessica said triumphantly, bursting into Elizabeth's room early Sunday morning.

"Haven't you ever heard of letting a person sleep late for a change?" Elizabeth mumbled, burrowing deeper in her blankets.

Jessica looked taken aback. "I was going to do the laundry," she said, hurt. "I just wanted to see if you had any clothes that needed washing."

"The laundry?" Elizabeth said incredulously, sitting straight up in bed and rubbing her eyes. "Are you serious? I don't think I've seen you do laundry in your life!"

"That," Jessica said merrily, "is because I've never done it! But there's no time like the present for learning how. Come on, Liz. Get out of bed so I can do your sheets."

"This is sick," Elizabeth said uneasily, looking at her twin as if she were deranged. "What's gotten into you, Jess?"

"We're entirely on our own!" Jessica sang out, tugging at her twin's sheets despite the fact that Elizabeth hadn't budged. "Entirely, completely on our own—and we can do whatever we like for an entire week, maybe longer!"

"Remember," Elizabeth said warningly, "that Mom and Dad called Steve and asked him to keep an eye on us if he could. He might come home any time. Besides—"

"What am I doing wrong?" Jessica demanded, looking injured. "I'm just trying to keep things tidy! Now, move it, Liz. I need the bottom sheet."

Elizabeth groaned and got out of bed. "I've got to get things ready for the talent show meeting here tonight. Are you going to be around, Jess?"

"Of course," Jessica said brightly, balling the sheets up and throwing them into the laundry basket. "DeeDee Gordon's coming, isn't she?" she asked innocently.

Elizabeth yawned. "God, I hope so," she muttered. "I'm really counting on her to get the sets all worked out."

"I'll be here," Jessica said sweetly, taking the laundry basket out of her sister's bedroom and closing the door behind her. *You can count on it!* she thought triumphantly. *I wouldn't miss seeing DeeDee tonight for the world.* Jessica had never forgiven DeeDee Gordon for stealing Bill Chase away from her. Not that Bill was that big a deal, really—but still. And then DeeDee had gone around telling everyone in the cast of the school play that her father, a big-time Hollywood agent, thought one of the actors he'd seen at a rehearsal was star material. Jessica had been sure he'd meant her. It had to have been! She'd practically had her home in Hollywood all picked out, when it turned out that *Bill* was the one Mr. Gordon was talking about. Jessica had been livid. First DeeDee had stolen Bill right out from under her nose, and then DeeDee's father yanked away her dream of becoming a movie star. No doubt about it, DeeDee needed to get a little of her own back. Jessica had been waiting for months for the perfect opportunity to get back at her.

And, as usual, fate had dropped DeeDee's punishment right into Jessica's lap! Maybe DeeDee already knew that Bill and Dana were at the movies together, Jessica mused. But if she did, she probably thought it was perfectly innocent. *Like Cara did*, she reminded herself. *But Cara's not interested in anything lately—she's getting kind of weird.*

With the right tone of voice and the right details thrown in, maybe I can help convince DeeDee of something completely different! Jessica thought, hurrying downstairs with the basket.

"Now, how in the world does this thing work?" Jessica muttered, staring at the washing machine. There were six buttons on top, and none of them said On or Off. "Don't overload machine," a warning read in small letters. "I wonder how much is considered overloading?" Jessica said, staring down at the pile of sheets and clothes she'd collected. After a minute's consideration, she jammed everything in, pouring in a healthy helping of soap flakes and pushing just about every button she could find. She thought the machine sounded a little strange, but then she'd never really listened to a washing machine before. Mrs. Wakefield usually did the wash. *You see*, Jessica thought triumphantly, bounding up the basement stairs, *I'm so much more independent with Mom and Dad away. I can tell this week is going to be really good for me!*

Next on the agenda was a cooking experiment. *Lila may think that guests are the only important part of a party*, Jessica thought, taking one of her mother's cookbooks off the shelf in the kitchen, *but I know better*. She had already decided to try out a recipe for miniature pizzas. They looked pretty easy, and if they turned out well, she could make a huge batch next Saturday morning.

"What are you doing?" Elizabeth asked suspiciously, coming in with the Sunday paper and turning on the kettle.

"I'm cooking. What does it look like?" Jessica said, wondering if her sister was suffering from a decline in intelligence. Wasn't it perfectly obvious what she was doing?

"Mushrooms?" Elizabeth asked, perplexed, watching Jessica pour oil into a frying pan and begin slicing vegetables on the cutting board.

"They're supposed to be sauteed," Jessica explained, "to go on top of the cheese and tomato. I'm making little pizzas."

"Oh," Elizabeth said blankly. "For breakfast? Wouldn't you rather have Cheerios or something?"

Jessica wiped her hands on the legs of her jeans and shook her head. "It's an *experiment*," she told her twin. "For the party next Saturday. If they work, I'm going to make—"

"Jessica," Elizabeth said ominously, putting up her hand, "what's that horrible clanking sound in the basement?"

"I don't know," Jessica said, her eyes widening.

The sound got worse when they opened the basement door. "God, it sounds *awful*," Jessica cried, hurrying down the steps. Elizabeth was right behind her. "I hope I didn't overload the machine," Jessica said.

"You didn't put all those sheets in, did you?" Elizabeth asked, alarmed. "Oh, God, Jess—"

By the time the twins got to the door of the laundry room, their worst fears were confirmed. Soap suds were pouring out under the door, and the dreadful clanking noise was so loud Elizabeth had to cover her ears with her hands. "Go in and turn it off!" she screamed.

"OK!" Jessica shouted back, pulling the door open. She couldn't believe the sight that greeted her. Soapy water was pouring out of the top of the machine, which was being lifted up each time the load inside spun around. Jessica plunged through the sea of suds, hurling herself on the lid. "Which one is the off button?" she hollered.

"The blue one!" Elizabeth screamed back.

Jessica pushed the blue button, and the terrible noise stopped after one last clank.

"Oh, dear," Jessica said, looking around her. "It's kind of wet in here. Do you suppose—"

"You broke it, Jess." Elizabeth moaned. "Plus there's enough water in here to drown an elephant! We're going to have to call the repairman tomorrow, and Mom's going to have a fit."

Jessica wasn't listening. Her aqua eyes wide with terror, she was sniffing the air, trying to place the faint smell of burning wafting down from the kitchen.

"The mushrooms!" she yelled, pushing Elizabeth aside and racing for the stairs, soap suds still clinging to her legs. The bottoms of her shoes were so wet she almost fell down twice. She reached the kitchen just in time. She had left the oil-filled frying pan on the burner, and it had caught fire. Grabbing a dish towel, she tried frantically to put out the flames, trying to remember what she'd learned in cooking class about grease fires. The towel promptly caught fire.

"Fire! Fire!" Elizabeth, who had followed her sister upstairs, was shrieking hysterically.

Just then the telephone rang.

Jessica burst into tears. "You get it, Liz!" she hollered, throwing the burning towel into the sink and dumping a whole canister of flour into the frying pan. Luckily the flour worked, putting out the flames. But Jessica was still shuddering as she picked up the charred black towel. The whole kitchen was filled with smoke, and her eyes were stinging dreadfully.

"It's Mom and Dad," Elizabeth said, covering the mouthpiece with her hand. Now that she saw everything was all right, a mischievous twinkle came to her eyes. "They just want to know if everything here is OK. What should I tell them?"

"Tell them," Jessica said grimly, flinging the kitchen window as far open as it would go, "that everything here is *fine*. In fact, it couldn't be better," she added, and she and Elizabeth both convulsed into hysterical giggles.

"It's nothing, Mom," Elizabeth said weakly into the phone a moment later, trying to control herself. "No, everything's fine. In fact," she added, winking at her twin, "we were just saying that things couldn't be any better here. Here's Jess. She'll tell you the same thing!"

"Liz is right, Mom," Jessica said, tossing the burned dish towel into the wastebasket. "Oh, yes," she confirmed solemnly, trying hard to keep a straight face as Elizabeth burst into giggles across the room. "We're taking perfect care of *everything*."

"I just wanted to remind you two that I left one of my floor plans for the Williams project on the drafting table in my study," Alice Wakefield said anxiously. "Don't let anything happen to it, OK?

It's the only copy we've got, and you know how important that account is to the firm!"

"Sure, Mom," Jessica said absentmindedly.

Boy, she was thinking. *I was off to such a good start this morning; now I've made a complete mess of everything!*

If I don't get the repairman to come in quickly, she thought, *it looks like I'm going to have to change the invitations for Saturday night and tell everyone it's going to be an indoor swimming party instead. Come dirty, leave clean. Do your laundry just by walking through the Wakefields' basement!*

It was all Jessica could do not to collapse with laughter while her mother told her what a wonderful time they were both having.

Thank goodness, Jessica thought. She was glad her parents weren't coming back for a while because it looked as if it was going to take her all week to get the house back to the way it had looked about an hour earlier!

"Hey, DeeDee," Jessica whispered, passing the dark-haired girl a bowl of potato chips, "will you come into the kitchen for a minute? I want to ask you about the set for the magic act."

"Sure," DeeDee said, looking surprised. She knew she wasn't a great favorite of Jessica Wakefield's.

Following Jessica, she got up and tiptoed out of the talent-show meeting, which was being held in the Wakefields' comfortable living room.

Elizabeth was talking to Ken and Winston about their act and didn't seem to mind their leaving.

"It's too bad Bill couldn't do his dramatic reading," Jessica said smoothly, sitting down at the kitchen table and pulling a chair out for DeeDee. "He's really a marvelous actor."

DeeDee flushed with pride. "That's nice of you to say," she murmured. "I wish he could be involved, too," she admitted wistfully. "But he's *so* busy these days! Swimming's taking up a lot of his time. And his work for Mr. Fellows—"

"I know," Jessica said. "That's why I was so surprised to run into him at the movies yesterday afternoon. He's amazing, really, taking on so much outside of his schoolwork and yet still finding time for W.C. Fields! That's what makes Bill so special, I think. He really *is* a well-rounded guy."

The color had been slowly draining from DeeDee's face. "You—you saw Bill yesterday at the movies?" she managed to get out. "Are you sure?"

Jessica could barely contain her joy. DeeDee hadn't known!

"Didn't you know?" she asked with theatrical surprise. "He was with Dana Larson. They looked like they were having *such* a good time. Actually, now that I think of it, I was kind of surprised he wasn't with *you*, since he has so little free time these days."

"Jessica," DeeDee said, standing up so fast the kitchen chair almost fell over, "could you tell Liz

69

that I had to leave early? I'll give her a call later on and find out what I missed, OK? I just remembered that I promised my mom I'd have the car home before nine."

"Go right ahead," Jessica said smoothly, feeling immensely satisfied as she watched DeeDee's face.

She'd never dreamed her plan would go so well. But from the look in DeeDee's eyes, Jessica had a feeling she'd succeeded beyond her wildest expectations.

She also had a feeling that wherever Bill Chase was that night, he was going to look as bad as DeeDee in about half an hour.

But after all, it isn't my fault, Jessica reassured herself as she hurried back into the meeting. *If Bill Chase had been more honest with his girlfriend, this little incident would never have happened!*

Seven

DeeDee had been trying to find Bill ever since Jessica told her about seeing him at the movies with Dana Larson. That had been the previous night, but Bill hadn't been at home when she called him.

Now, Monday morning, DeeDee was struggling to sit still through her classes. But all she could think about was Bill and Dana. *What an idiot I've been*, she thought despondently. *I knew he'd been acting weird—and this is obviously why.*

DeeDee had been waiting for something like this to happen. But she'd had no idea how rotten it would make her feel. She hadn't slept a wink the night before, and she knew she looked horrible that morning. How could she sleep? How would she ever be able to do anything again? Bill had been her whole life.

I have nothing left, DeeDee thought woefully. *Nothing.*

The bell rang, and she got up listlessly, picking

up her books and papers and shuffling toward the door. To her surprise, Bill was waiting for her outside the classroom. "My mom says you called last night," he said cheerfully, giving her a quick kiss on the cheek, "and I felt bad about not being able to call back. I went to Mr. Fellows's house—"

I'll bet, DeeDee thought viciously. *I'll just bet.*

"Hey," Bill said suddenly, noticing her expression. "What's wrong?"

"Oh, *nothing*," DeeDee said bitterly. "I guess I just sort of thought that you and I were honest with each other, Bill. I mean, if you had a reason for lying to me I could understand it. But—"

"What are you talking about?" Bill demanded, his blue eyes narrowing. They had been walking down the crowded hall together, but now Bill grabbed DeeDee's arm and steered her toward the student lounge, which Bill was pleased to see was empty. He shut the door behind them and turned to face DeeDee, his expression darkening. "Now, would you mind telling me what's going on?" he demanded.

"If you," DeeDee choked, "would just mind telling me what you were doing with Dana Larson at the movies on Saturday afternoon. You *told* me you were at the library, and I believed you—"

"Oh, God," Bill groaned, pulling DeeDee to him and putting his arms around her. "I was afraid this might happen! But you see, it was only because I thought you'd make such a big deal out of nothing that I didn't tell you!''

"You mean it's true?" DeeDee gasped, tears spilling down her pale cheeks. "Bill, how could you? Why would you do something like that to me?"

"It was nothing," Bill said, looking completely confused. "Honestly! Dana had tickets to a W.C. Fields movie, and she asked me to go with her! That's it—the whole story."

"Why didn't you tell me?" DeeDee sobbed. "You didn't want me to find out!" she added accusingly.

"No," Bill said and sighed. "I didn't. But only because you've been acting so strange lately that I thought it might upset you. DeeDee, Dana is only a friend, nothing more."

"I'll bet!" DeeDee said furiously. "Are you going to do anything with her again?" she asked, brushing the angry tears from her eyes.

"I don't know," Bill said defensively. "Since when do I have to ask you for permission to do everything? That isn't the way we used to operate!"

"I bet you *will* see her again," DeeDee said hysterically. She couldn't believe it. She really was losing him. And nothing she could do or say seemed to make him understand.

"Maybe I will," Bill said angrily. "I have every right to, Dee. She's a *friend!* I just don't understand what's gotten into you these days!"

"You don't understand anything!" DeeDee

shrieked. The minute the words left her mouth she wished she hadn't said them. She could see now how angry Bill was. It was all her fault—again.

"Maybe I don't," Bill muttered, his teeth clenched. "I sure as hell don't understand what's gotten into you, Dee. And all I can say is that the way things are going, I think it's time we called it quits."

The next thing DeeDee knew, Bill had stormed out of the lounge, leaving her alone, her brown eyes shining with tears.

DeeDee had never felt so terrible in her life. It was like the day her father had left, only worse—a million times worse.

She felt as though she had lost her only friend in the world, and she had no idea what was going to keep her going. Too weak to move from the lounge, she sank down onto one of the couches, burying her head in her arms, and began to sob.

Just then Elizabeth walked into the lounge, "DeeDee!" she said, startled. "What's wrong? You look terrible!"

"Thanks," DeeDee said wryly, lifting her tear-streaked face.

"I'm sorry," Elizabeth said quickly, covering her mouth with her hand. "Do you want to be alone? If—"

"No," DeeDee murmured, wiping her face with a tissue. "Actually, I could really use a shoulder to cry on, Liz."

"Did something happen between you and Bill?" Elizabeth asked gently. "I just saw him rushing down the hall, and he looked kind of miserable, too."

DeeDee's stomach turned over. Just hearing Bill's name made her experience the whole terrible argument all over again.

"We broke up," she whispered, taking a long, gulping breath of air. Strangely enough, the minute she'd said it she felt a little bit better. Better enough to tell Elizabeth what had happened, anyway. She didn't tell Elizabeth that Jessica was the one who had told her about Bill and Dana. That seemed impolite. But she told her everything else.

Elizabeth looked sympathetic and concerned. "That doesn't sound like Bill," she mused. "You mean he went to the movies with Dana without telling you, and then didn't understand when you got upset!"

DeeDee nodded. "It was horrible," she confessed. "Gosh, Liz, I don't know what I'm going to do without him!"

"Well," Elizabeth suggested, "maybe you were just both really upset, too upset to make sense. Have you thought about finding Bill once you're calmer and talking the whole thing out? That's happened to Todd and me," she admitted. "When you're both really upset, you just can't think. Maybe Bill feels as bad as you do right now."

A tiny glimmer of hope flared up in DeeDee's

heart. "Do you think so, Liz?" she asked eagerly. She wanted so badly to believe Elizabeth!

If only she could convince Bill to make a clean start, DeeDee thought. It wouldn't matter then about Dana—or anything! Their whole problem had started because DeeDee had been so afraid of losing him. And *now* look what she'd done!

Thanking Elizabeth, DeeDee hurried out of the lounge. Maybe she could find Bill in the cafeteria, she told herself. Maybe she could convince him to give her another chance.

She refused to let herself consider what would happen if Bill didn't *want* to try again. That, as far as DeeDee was concerned, was a possibility too bleak even to consider.

Bill was sitting at a table with Winston Egbert and Ken Matthews, looking suspiciously at the meat loaf on his tray. "This stuff looks kind of weird," he muttered, probing it with his fork.

"Maybe we can use it in our magic act, Ken," Winston mumbled, his mouth full of mashed potatoes. "The amazing, the wonderful, the fabulous—meat loaf! Guaranteed to turn a normal, healthy, red-blooded junior into a shivering basket case!"

"Ho-ho, Egbert," Bill said cheerlessly. "You really crack me up."

Bill felt peculiar, sitting in the lunchroom without DeeDee. He had to admit he missed her—badly, in fact.

But at the same time he couldn't help feeling a little relieved. The incident had heightened for Bill all the emotions he'd been feeling these last few weeks—the depression, the anxiety, the exhaustion. DeeDee had just become too hard to deal with. She'd lost most of her spark. She had given up all of the things that had made her such an individual, and she was so dependent on him that it terrified him. He didn't want a girlfriend who was like a millstone around his neck! He wanted someone who was his equal—someone like DeeDee when he'd first met her, he thought sadly.

But not DeeDee as she was now.

"Hey," Winston said suddenly, "your girlfriend approaches. Should Matthews and I get lost?"

Bill turned his head. Sure enough, DeeDee was making her way between the crowded tables and chairs, trying to get to the table where he was sitting. "I'll go talk to her," Bill mumbled, leaving his lunch behind. He didn't want DeeDee to make a scene in front of his friends.

"Dee!" he called. "Why don't we go outside," he suggested when he made it over to her. "OK? We can talk out there."

"Thanks, Bill," DeeDee said gratefully.

He looked at her closely, surprised by the tone of her voice. Actually she didn't look bad. Her eyes were swollen, but he couldn't really tell if she'd been crying. "How are you?" he asked, really wanting to know.

"OK," she said softly, looking down at the ground. "I want to talk things over with you," she told him when they were finally outside, sitting alone together on the grass. "I feel awful about this morning. Bill, I want to make things work."

Bill flushed, picking at a piece of grass. "DeeDee, you know how much I care for you," he began.

"Please," DeeDee interrupted, as if she sensed what he was about to say and wanted to fend off his response. "Just hear me out, OK?"

"OK," Bill said, smiling gently at her.

"Look," DeeDee said, obviously struggling to make the words come out, "I know I've been acting strangely lately. And I'm not entirely sure myself what the reasons are. I think somehow I've just gotten really terrified of losing you, so I've been hanging on too hard. And at the same time I've felt you withdrawing, acting colder and more distant."

"Maybe that's true," Bill admitted. "It's been a hard time for me. I guess I've had more demands on my time than usual, and maybe I'm not experienced enough to be able to balance all the things I'm doing. I'm sorry, Dee. I never meant to hurt you."

"Don't you think we still have a chance?" DeeDee asked, tears in her eyes.

Bill took a deep breath. *Remember how it's been for the last few weeks*, he told himself. *Like at the swim meet. Or at the Chinese restaurant. I want a girlfriend*, he reminded himself. *Not a noose around my neck.*

"I don't know, Dee," he said slowly. "Maybe in a little while we could try again, after we've both given it some time. Right now I just feel like I need time to myself, time to straighten everything out. I've been so confused."

DeeDee bit her lip, struggling not to cry. She had to be calm, she told herself. She had to sound reasonable. Otherwise, she'd lose him forever.

"Look," she argued, "let's try again. *Now.* I promise I'll be more understanding about your schedule. I won't be so dependent on you. I know I've been a pain in the neck lately, but I swear it will be different if you just give me a chance."

Bill got to his feet, avoiding her gaze so his resolve wouldn't weaken. He just wasn't ready to be shackled again. He wanted to see how it felt to be free—entirely free.

And he couldn't help distrusting DeeDee a little. He knew her intentions couldn't be better, but it had been so hard lately. Was she really ready to give him more space? Or would she continue to smother him, continue to make him feel trapped?

"I'm sorry, Dee," he said gently. "I just need some more time." Kneeling down, he kissed her gently on the top of her head, trying not to notice the tears running down her cheeks.

He had a feeling he would never forget the

look on DeeDee's face as he turned to walk away. *But I've got to do it*, he told himself, taking a long, quavering breath as he walked away from her across the lawn. *DeeDee's got to learn to stand on her own two feet again. And I'm afraid as long as she's got me to lean on, that just isn't going to happen.*

Eight

It was Tuesday afternoon, and Elizabeth was on her hands and knees in the school gym, helping DeeDee with the lettering for Winston and Ken's magic act. The gym was filled with activity. Olivia Davidson was taking Patty Gilbert's measurements in one corner and discussing what sort of costume would be best for her dance routine. Mr. Collins was showing Ken how to set up the audio equipment, and Todd was experimenting with the spotlight.

"Liz, can you help me with the backdrop for Patty's dance later?" DeeDee begged. "I'm really nervous about it. I've got other people working on some of the other sets but I want to do that one myself. And I want it to be absolutely perfect."

Patty was doing a short dance to a piece of music from *West Side Story*, and DeeDee wanted the set to be "something that gives the whole dance a mood."

Elizabeth sat back, wiping her forehead with a dusty hand. "I don't know, Dee," she said honestly. "It looks like I'm really busy this afternoon. Do you think you can get started on your own? I'd be happy to tell you what I think once you've got it underway."

DeeDee went pale. "I'll never be able to do it by myself!" she wailed.

"Can't you get someone else who's helping you with the sets to work on it?" When DeeDee vigorously shook her head no, Elizabeth sighed, "OK, OK. Let me go to see how Todd's doing with the lighting. I'll get back to you as soon as I can."

"What's wrong?" Todd demanded, putting down the cord he'd been repairing. "You look about as frazzled as this lighting system does!"

"It's DeeDee," Elizabeth whispered, slipping her arm through Todd's. "She's driving me crazy! Todd, the girl can't do one single thing by herself. I had to find people to help paint sets. Do you realize she's called me four times since she and Bill broke up? And that was only yesterday!"

"Poor Liz," Todd said sympathetically, giving her a hug. "I guess everyone's dumping their problems on you these days, huh?"

Elizabeth shook her head. "No one but DeeDee," she demurred. "Boy, I can see now how Bill must've felt," she continued. "Todd, that girl has absolutely *no* self-esteem. She called twice last night to talk about Bill. She wanted to know how I thought she could get him to come back to her. I told her the only thing I could—that she'd just have to accept his decision and get used to it. *Then* she started calling about the talent show. She's so panicked about doing even the simplest little thing without asking me what I think about it. Honestly, Todd, it would have been easier for me to go ahead and do the sets myself!"

"Hey," Todd said warningly, "I think you're about to get nailed again. DeeDee's coming over here, and from the look on her face, I have a feeling she needs help again."

"Oh, no," Elizabeth moaned.

"Liz!" DeeDee called, hurrying across the gym. "I've got an idea for Patty's set, but I feel uncertain about it. Do you think you could come over and look at the plans I've drawn up for it?"

"Sure." Elizabeth sighed and shook her head at Todd as she went off with DeeDee.

"I'm sorry to keep bugging you," DeeDee said. "But it's been so long since I've done this sort of thing, and I really want it all to be good. I wish I knew more about design," she added self-deprecatingly.

"DeeDee," Elizabeth said firmly, "you know more than anyone in this whole room does about it, including me. Don't you realize that you're a very talented girl?"

DeeDee looked blankly at Elizabeth.

She doesn't understand, Elizabeth thought. *God knows why, but she just has no idea how capable she is.*

Or maybe, Elizabeth thought with a flash of

insight, she *did* know, but she wanted to be helpless and dependent on people. But why in the world would she want that?

"What I wanted to do," DeeDee murmured self-consciously, leading Elizabeth over to the tiny area where she'd been sketching designs, "was to convey the mood of a poor neighborhood in New York City. But I wanted a romantic feeling, too. So I thought something like this." Picking up her sketchbook, DeeDee showed Elizabeth her plan: a backdrop of a tenement and a vacant lot, beautifully rendered with simple lines. "What do you think?" DeeDee asked breathlessly. "We'll need lighting, of course, to soften the effect and make it more romantic. And—"

She stopped suddenly, as if aware that she was sounding more commanding, more sure of herself. "What do you think, Liz?" she asked in a very small voice.

Elizabeth shook her head admiringly. "It's wonderful," she told her. "Almost too wonderful for a school talent show. You're really good, Dee."

"Oh, it's nothing," DeeDee mumbled. "Liz, are you going to be home later on this evening?" she asked shyly, her eyes on the ground. "I was wondering if we could talk for a few minutes . . . you know, about—"

"Liz!" Todd called, holding up the spotlight. "I need your help, pronto!"

Elizabeth bit her lip. "I'm sorry, Dee," she said

softly, "but tonight's going to be a madhouse. Maybe I can—"

"Never mind," DeeDee said. "Some other time, OK?"

Elizabeth took a deep breath as she walked back across the gym to join Todd and Winston. *I don't know what's wrong with that girl,* she thought to herself, *but I have a feeling I was a little too quick to criticize Bill for breaking up with her.* Elizabeth had the impression now there was a lot more to the whole thing than just the incident with Dana. *Because if DeeDee is hanging onto me this much,* Elizabeth reasoned, *just think how impossible she must have been with poor Bill!*

DeeDee needed—well, Elizabeth didn't know *what* she needed. She sighed. Maybe DeeDee needed to realize how much she had going for her. And she needed to be able to stand on her own two feet, to be her own person. Because until then, Elizabeth thought, there was no way Bill Chase was going to want her back.

And even more important, there was no way DeeDee was going to be happy—either by herself, or as a part of a couple—until she learned to value herself and to do things without always having to lean on somebody else.

In despair DeeDee looked down at the plans she'd sketched. They still weren't right, she thought miserably. If only there were someone around she could ask for advice; if only Bill . . .

She tried to blink her tears away. She knew she had to forget Bill.

DeeDee was working especially hard on this set because it was for Patty. Maybe a good design would make things better between her and her friend, DeeDee thought wistfully. She took a large sheet of poster board and began to mark it with a pencil to get a sense of the right dimensions for the sketch of the tenement building.

DeeDee was acutely aware that Patty was disappointed in her. How could she help but be? DeeDee thought harshly. She had behaved like such a jerk around Patty for the last month or two. Patty expected the world of her. She expected DeeDee to be as good at everything as she was.

Well, I'm just not, DeeDee thought, a lump forming in her throat. *They're all disappointed in me—Patty, Bill, Elizabeth . . .*

If only she could make them all happy, do what they wanted her to do.

But she just couldn't.

Everywhere she looked, DeeDee saw bright, capable, energetic people. They made her feel so jealous—so overwhelmed.

The strange thing was that DeeDee knew that at one point *she* had been that way. She'd signed up for projects without worrying about whether or not she could do them well. She'd taken charge of projects, tried new sports, and none of it had seemed scary or intimidating.

Well, she didn't know what had changed, but something was definitely different now. *Maybe because you used to do things that you wanted to do*, a little voice inside her suggested. You *liked theater, so you joined the drama club.* You *wanted to learn to surf so you asked Bill for lessons.* You *wanted to learn more about design, so you signed up for courses.*

Tears rushed to DeeDee's eyes. In a flash she realized how different she had become. Somehow she had begun seeing herself only in comparison to other people, or only as fulfillments of their wishes—or disappointments to them. She had stopped thinking of herself as her own person. All that mattered now was what other people thought of her, how much she was letting them down.

Bit by bit she'd lost her confidence. As soon as she saw art as something others expected her to be good at, she had balked. She forgot how much she loved to draw, to design things. All she could focus on was how much people expected of her—demanded of her, it seemed.

And then there was Bill. Bill had everything—looks, talent, brains. He was so confident about everything he did, and DeeDee had always backed him in everything. It wasn't Bill's fault, but gradually she had begun to spend more and more time concentrating on what *he* was doing. If Bill had swim practice, she found herself skipping art classes to sit up in the bleachers and watch him. At first Bill had reveled in all the attention. Later he had begun to get nervous, telling her she needed to find things to do on her own.

DeeDee sat straight up, the color draining from her face as she realized the conclusion she was coming to. It wasn't just her fault, she thought, almost giddy with relief. Bill had been to blame, too. He'd enjoyed all the attention he was getting—and in part he might even have been glad that she was dropping activities to spend more time with him. Things had gone too far, though, and he wasn't glad at all anymore. He felt suffocated. *But it wasn't just her fault. Bill was involved too.*

DeeDee felt as if an enormous weight had been lifted from her. It seemed that for the last couple of years—since her parents' divorce—all she'd been doing was blaming herself for things. She felt apprehensive when something wonderful happened because she was afraid she'd spoil it.

When Bill had fallen in love with her, the anxiety had started all over again. She became convinced she was going to lose him. *And I made sure I did*, DeeDee realized, shaking her head as she recalled her behavior over the last week or two. It was as if she had been so afraid of losing happiness that she'd wanted to lose it quickly, to control the agony she knew was going to come sooner or later.

DeeDee knew enough about the way divorce can affect children to recognize that some of the emotions she'd been experiencing were normal.

"But what about my loss of confidence?" she wondered aloud, staring down at the preliminary sketches she'd made. "And more important, how am I going to pull myself together and be able to take charge of things again, the way I could once?"

"Patty," Elizabeth said in a low, urgent voice, "can I give you a ride home? I really need to talk to you."

"Sure, Liz," Patty said, slipping her arms into her navy blazer. She had just changed from her leotard back into a skirt and blouse, and as always Elizabeth was amazed by how perfectly put together she looked.

"What's up?" Patty asked, following Elizabeth out to the parking lot and slipping into the passenger seat of the red Fiat Spider.

"I'm sure you can guess." Elizabeth sighed and shook her head. "I just don't know what to do about DeeDee. I've got my hands full right now, and I don't have time to help her out. Besides, I don't know a thing about sets. She's so talented, but she's got *no* confidence. Honestly, I'm getting a little anxious. We've got so little time left, and—"

"Oh, dear." Patty sighed. "I was afraid something like this might happen. Have you tried talking to her about it?"

Elizabeth nodded emphatically, her blond ponytail bouncing as she backed the Fiat out of its parking space. "No luck," she admitted. "She just won't listen to reason!"

"It's really kind of strange," Patty mused. "DeeDee's never had much of a problem when it came to her self-confidence. Ever since she was a little kid she's been a real leader—always at the head of everything."

"What do you suppose made her change so much?" Elizabeth asked.

Patty shrugged. "She's just going through a bad period," she said. "Who knows—maybe it has something to do with her parents splitting up. Maybe not. Mostly I think it has to do with Bill. DeeDee's never been in love before, and she's fallen pretty hard. She's having a hard time balancing her feelings for him with her feelings of self-esteem. I think she'll be all right eventually—DeeDee always lands on her feet. But right now . . ."

"Right now?" Elizabeth prompted.

Patty burst out laughing. "Right now we need a good plan to keep DeeDee from driving you up a wall. Who knows," she added, her brown eyes lighting up as if something had just occurred to her, "maybe we could kill two birds with one stone."

"What do you mean?" Elizabeth asked, intrigued.

"What we need," Patty mused, "is a way to make DeeDee realize that she really *is* capable of handling a lot of pressure and doing an excellent job at something that's entirely her own—

something that has nothing to do with you or me or Bill Chase or anyone but DeeDee. Right?''

"Right," Elizabeth agreed.

"And at the same time we need to get DeeDee off your back so you can put the talent show together. Right?''

"Right!" Elizabeth said, wondering what Patty was getting at.

"Elizabeth Wakefield," Patty said, a wide smile spreading over her dark face, "I have just come up with a plan that's going to accomplish both these things beyond your wildest expectations!"

And, a mischievous smile on her pretty face, she proceeded to fill Elizabeth in on the details.

Nine

"Let's see," Jessica said, tucking her legs underneath her on the couch in the living room and scanning the list in her hand. "I've called the Patmans, and Roger and Bruce can both come. Lila's calling Drake, and he's going to ask a couple of his friends from Delta Theta, or whatever it's called. Aaron Dallas, Cara Walker, Ken Matthews, Neil Freemount . . . Bill Chase!" she said suddenly, a wicked gleam in her eye. She'd forgotten when she dropped the bomb on DeeDee Gordon that she was creating one more eligible male for her guest list. "And Cara . . . I wonder what to do about Cara."

Jessica was beginning to worry about her best friend. For as long as she could remember, Cara had been wonderful company—as keen as Jessica was on things like cheerleading, shopping, parties, and gossip. Lately all that had changed. Cara was much quieter than usual, almost withdrawn. When Jessica asked her about it, all Cara would say was that there were some problems at home. Jessica had had to work unusually hard to get at the truth. The Walkers were talking about separating—maybe even a divorce.

"I'll invite her," Jessica decided, making a note on her pad, though Cara hadn't been much fun at parties lately. Jessica sighed. "And maybe Liz and Todd . . ."

"Liz and Todd what?" Elizabeth demanded, coming into the room and unceremoniously dumping a pile of paper on the carpet. "Boy, just look at all this stuff," she complained . "My arms are getting longer just from carting around these talent show plans all the time!"

"Liz," Jessica said seriously, "are you and Todd going to come Saturday night? I need to know so I can plan how much food we're going to need."

"You're not really serious about having a party here, are you?" Elizabeth demanded. "Come on, Jess. We've finally got the place looking normal again! As it is we've got a bill for seventy-five dollars from the washing-machine man."

"Nothing's going to happen," Jessica said defensively. "For heaven's sake, Liz. You think I'm such a child!"

"It isn't *you* I'm worried about," Elizabeth said darkly. "It's the people on your guest list. Remember what happened when Steve had a party here that time Mom and Dad were away?"

"Steve's friends were a bunch of animals,"

Jessica said, miffed. "Come on, Liz. It won't be any fun if you and Todd aren't here."

"Todd's been kind of down lately," Elizabeth said thoughtfully, her eyes darkening. "In fact, I'm a little worried about him. I wonder . . ."

Maybe it would be a good thing if they did go to the party, she was thinking. Lately the time they'd spent alone together had been kind of hard. Todd seemed depressed about something, but he wouldn't tell her what it was. Maybe it would do him good to be with a bunch of people. It just might cheer him up.

"He just needs some fun," Jessica chimed in, echoing her twin's own thoughts. "Come on, Liz."

"All right." Elizabeth sighed. "Todd's supposed to come over tonight after dinner to help me with my math, and I'll ask him then."

"Hooray!" Jessica shouted, jumping up and throwing her arms around her sister. "You're the most wonderful twin in the whole wide world!"

"But remember," Elizabeth said warningly, "we've got to be incredibly careful. Didn't Mom and Dad say they might be coming home earlier than they'd planned when they called last night?"

"Oh, they won't come home early," Jessica said dismissively, reaching for the phone. "They said it's gorgeous down there, and Mom's having the time of her life! Why would they want to come home *early*?"

Elizabeth laughed. "Hey, tell me when you're

done with the phone," she called, gathering her papers together and heading for the stairs. "I need to call DeeDee, OK?"

"OK!" Jessica yelled back, dialing Lila Fowler's number.

"Did you get through to Drake?" Jessica asked Lila after the maid had called her to the phone.

Lila sounded dazed. "I just woke up," she complained. "I've been lying down in a darkened room every afternoon with cucumber slices on my eyelids. It prevents puffiness."

Jessica shook her head in disbelief. "Who cares about your *eyelids*?" she demanded. "I want to know if you called Drake or not. You said you were going to, Lila. And instead, all you do is lie around with vegetables on your face."

"I called him." Lila yawned. "Don't get so excited. Daddy's thinking of sending me to a spa for my birthday this year," she confided. "They have this marvelous machine at the Fountain of Youth that takes all the fat off the backs of your thighs. And they soak you in minerals until you're entirely purified."

"Lila!" Jessica shrieked. "I don't *care* about the backs of your thighs. What did Drake say?"

"He's coming, he's coming," Lila drawled. "Just relax. You're probably straining your voice and getting little lines on the sides of your mouth. That's what this new beauty book I just bought says. Supposedly—"

"Lila," Jessica fumed, teeth clenched, "I don't

care what your beauty book says. Tell me about Drake. Are any of his friends coming?"

"Of course," Lila said. "He said he was going to put up a notice in his fraternity, so a few people ought to turn up."

"He what?" Jessica gasped. "He put a sign up? Lila, I thought you said—"

"Don't worry," Lila reassured her. "No more than three or four will turn up, honest. Drake says they have midterms next week and everyone's going to be really busy."

"God, I hope so," Jessica said. She had a vision of hordes of college guys stampeding all over the house.

Suddenly she didn't feel very cheerful.

I hope Elizabeth isn't right, she thought. *Mom and Dad better not come home early. Because from the way things sound, it's going to look like World War III around this place on Sunday morning!*

"DeeDee?" Elizabeth said into the phone. "It's Liz."

"Oh, hi," DeeDee said. "I was just about to call you. Liz, what do you think I should do about the magic-act set? I wanted to use just a black sheet, but I thought—"

"DeeDee," Elizabeth said, trying to make her voice sound gravelly, "the reason I called is that I'm sick. I've got a fever," she said pointedly. "I just called my doctor, and he says I can go to school tomorrow but I have to come straight home afterward. So I was wondering if you could take charge of the meeting for me tomorrow afternoon."

"Me?" DeeDee said, shocked. "Oh, Liz, I couldn't possibly! I don't know the first thing about half this stuff! I—are you really feeling bad?" she asked. "That's awful, Liz! The talent show's this Sunday night!"

"I know," Elizabeth croaked. "Believe me, I know. That's why I've got to skip the meeting tomorrow. With any luck if I go to bed early tonight, I'll be all better by Friday. The doctor thinks it's probably just a twenty-four-hour bug of some sort. But—"

"Oh, Liz," DeeDee said, "I can't possibly take over the meeting! What if something went wrong or—what about Patty?" she demanded. "She'd be perfect! She's got tons of experience, and she's so good at organizing people!"

"Patty can't make it tomorrow," Elizabeth said mournfully. "She's got a dentist appointment right after school."

"Oh," DeeDee said, sounding disappointed. "Oh, Lord. Well, what about Todd? He knows a lot about this sort of thing, and—"

"Mr. Collins asked me to ask *you*," Elizabeth said pointedly, hoping the white lie would work. "As the person in charge of sets, you're second in command, DeeDee. I really need your help."

"Oh." DeeDee hesitated. "Well, OK then. What should I—"

"It'll all be fine," Elizabeth told her, cutting

her off on purpose. "Just take charge of things as best you can. I know you can do it, Dee."

"Well," DeeDee said doubtfully, "I hope so. But it's just for tomorrow," she added, as if trying to reassure herself. "OK. Well, feel better, Liz. Get lots of sleep. And—"

"I will," Elizabeth said abruptly. "I'll give you a call tomorrow night to find out what I missed, OK?"

"OK," DeeDee said weakly.

Elizabeth bit her lip as she hung up the phone. *Poor DeeDee*, she thought guiltily. *I hope Patty's right. I hope this is the way to show DeeDee she can do it! But it seems so hard on her!*

A minute later the phone rang. It was Patty.

"How did Operation A-Independence go?" Patty joked.

"Fine," Elizabeth told her. "Did you get through to Mr. Collins?"

"He's a little worried about it," Patty admitted. "But, yes, he agreed to the whole thing. I convinced him that DeeDee will do an excellent job. And now all we can do is keep our fingers crossed and just hope I'm right about DeeDee."

"She'll pull through," Elizabeth said, wishing she were as confident about the girl's ability as she sounded.

Patty's plan was a good one, she thought—if it worked. But if it didn't, more than DeeDee's self-esteem was at stake. The entire talent show was depending on DeeDee now.

Elizabeth just wasn't sure the girl would be

able to handle it. But all she could do now was hold her breath and pray.

The rest, Elizabeth thought, *is up to DeeDee*.

Elizabeth and Todd were sitting in the living room, their math homework spread out before them. "I understood it all pretty well up till chapter thirty-five," Elizabeth told him. "And then everything got sort of confusing."

Todd was staring at her, a funny expression in his brown eyes. "Liz, do you have any idea how beautiful you are?" he whispered, touching her tenderly on the cheek.

"What brought that on?" she teased him, leaning forward to give him a quick kiss. "I guess math is more romantic than I ever dreamed!"

"No," Todd said, his face clouding over, "it's just that sometimes . . . I don't know, I think about losing you . . ."

"Todd, what are you talking about?" Elizabeth demanded. "Why in the world would you ever lose me?"

Todd bit his lip. "Never mind," he whispered. "OK," he said abruptly, clearing his throat. "Chapter thirty-five, right?"

"Todd!" Elizabeth begged. "Tell me what's been bugging you. I just can't stand it any more. You seem so sad!"

"It's nothing," Todd said firmly. "Can't a guy get sentimental these days? Or does there have to be a good reason for it?"

Elizabeth stared at him. Was he telling the truth, or was something really wrong?

She didn't know. But Todd didn't seem like his old self to her. He seemed moody, sad, and reflective, as if he were contemplating something too enormous even to share with her.

I just wish I knew what it was, she thought. *Todd's always been able to confide in me. It isn't like him to keep something bottled up inside.*

Unless, she thought uneasily, it was too awful to talk about. But what in the world could have happened that was so dreadful?

Holding Todd's hand tightly with her own, Elizabeth reluctantly turned back to her math book. She didn't know what could possibly be the matter, but she promised herself that as soon as the talent show was over, she was going to do everything she could to find out what was wrong with Todd.

Ten

DeeDee was downstairs in the basement, putting the finishing touches on the backdrop for Patty's *West Side Story* dance number. She took a deep breath, then stepped back and regarded the flat. It was finished!

"It's wonderful," she said aloud, her brown eyes widening with amazement.

She had painted the tenement buildings brown, and the yellow paint she had used to evoke lit-up rooms in the darkness of the city night had worked perfectly. It was the most illustrative set she had ever done, and DeeDee felt her heartbeat quicken as she stood back from her work, admiring her efforts.

"DeeDee!" her mother called. "The phone's for you! It's Bill," she added, covering the receiver with her hand.

DeeDee looked blankly at the flat in front of her, her brow wrinkling. "Ask him if I can call him back," she called without stopping to think.

If I add one little bit of red right here, she was think-ing, *the colors will look terrific with the spotlight on them, and it'll pick up the red scarf Patty will be wearing.*

A minute later her mother came downstairs. She had a puzzled expression on her face. "That was a surprise," she remarked. "For Bill, too! I thought you were so anxious to talk to him, sweetie."

DeeDee was concentrating so hard on her work that it took her a moment to realize the enormity of what she'd just done. "God, I must be an idiot!" she cried, slapping herself on the forehead. "I've been hoping he'd call for days! This talent-show business is driving me crazy." She laughed. "I barely know which end is up anymore!"

"Dee, this is wonderful!" her mother gasped, standing in front of the completed set. "It's abso-lutely fabulous. No wonder you didn't want to leave it to talk on the phone!"

"It's been a long time since I've done some-thing I liked this much," DeeDee admitted.

"You know," DeeDee's mother said, sinking down into a chair near the table where her daughter was working, "I've always been a little jealous of both you and your father. You're both so strongly centered on one particular interest. I always felt as though I was floundering a bit."

DeeDee stared at her mother in amazement. It had never occurred to her that other people suf-fered from insecurity the same way she did—

especially someone like her mother, who always seemed so sure of herself!

"Daddy's like that," DeeDee admitted. "But not me. I don't know what I want to do! I'm not even very sure if I have any talents."

But DeeDee's face burned as she said that. She knew she had been fibbing. She just wanted her mother to protest and say that it wasn't true. Because DeeDee *did* know she had talent. She couldn't have put together a set like this if she hadn't.

"Dee," her mother said, shaking her head, "don't make the mistake of selling yourself short. There'll be people enough out there who will do that for you at some point. If you're not willing to champion yourself, you're ten paces back from the very start!"

DeeDee bit her lip. There was something she wanted to ask her mother, something she'd wanted to ask her for a long time. Ever since the day Ms. Jackson took her out for lunch and told her about her divorce.

"Mom," she asked hesitantly, "did you ever feel like you might have hung onto Dad if you hadn't been so strong-willed? Maybe if you hadn't gone back to school, or started to work . . ."

Her mother looked at her very seriously, her brown eyes thoughtful. "It's very hard to be sure what causes two people to split up, Dee," she said softly. "After what you and Bill have been through, I'm sure you'd agree with that. Maybe

105

at first I blamed our schedules, but I was kidding myself. Our divorce didn't have anything to do with your father's work *or* mine. We both changed a great deal, and we began to feel we'd each be happier on our own. What I *do* know," she said very slowly, as if she wanted DeeDee to realize how important her words were, "is that I would've gone crazy after the divorce if it weren't for the courses I was taking. I wasn't as passionate about being a social worker as you are about your design work. But it was something of my own, something to hang onto. I felt at first as if your father had taken away everything—my identity, my status, my whole reason for existing. Without something of my own to care about I would never have made it."

DeeDee's eyes stung with tears. *I never understood*, she thought numbly. It was probably the same with Susan Jackson, too. Her work probably didn't break up her marriage at all! She may have believed it did. But if so, she was wrong.

I've been such a jerk, she thought. *Such an absolute jerk.*

"What is it, sweetie?" her mother asked as DeeDee flung her arms around her, sniffling into her neck.

"Nothing," DeeDee mumbled, hanging on as if she'd never let go. She was crying, but she didn't feel sad. She felt as if she had come out of a long, dark tunnel and suddenly she could see things clearly again.

"You know," she said, lifting her tear-streaked face and giving her mother a final hug, "as soon as this talent show is over, I think I'm going to give Ms. Jackson a call and see if I can start taking those design classes again. What do you think of that?"

"That," her mother said, a look of enormous relief spreading over her face, "is just about the best news I've heard in ages!"

DeeDee, drawing in a long, quavering breath and turning back to look at the set she'd done for Patty, thought so too.

"What do you mean, the sound system doesn't work?" DeeDee demanded, looking hysterical. The talent-show committee was gathered in the auditorium, and DeeDee was doing her best to supervise the pandemonium. It seemed as though the perfect order of all Elizabeth's plans had completely crumbled overnight.

"I hate to do this to you, Dee," Todd added, "but the lighting system's shot, too. We're really messed up."

"OK," DeeDee said. "The sets are all taken care of. The sound system is broken. The light system is broken. What else?"

"Costumes." Olivia Davidson moaned. "My sewing machine broke down last night, and I've still got four costumes to finish! DeeDee, will you go ask someone in the home economics department if I can use one of theirs?"

DeeDee felt sick. How was she supposed to

take care of everything at once? It all looked so easy when Elizabeth was in charge.

"Disaster!" Winston Egbert yelled as he came charging into the gym almost half an hour late for the meeting. "Complete and utter disaster! My mom's on the PTA board, and she told me today that they've got a meeting scheduled here for Sunday night. Did anyone clear the use of the auditorium for Sunday evening?"

"That's right," Ken Matthews said, horror-stricken. "And we've got to figure out who's going to sell tickets, and—"

"Stop!" DeeDee shrieked, covering her ears with both hands. "OK, look," she said, trying her best to stay calm. "Let's meet again tomorrow at the same time. By then Liz will be all better, and she knows how to handle this stuff a million times better than I do. Meanwhile, I'll get going on as much of this stuff as I can. And I guess you guys should just start rehearsing. OK?"

No one looked very reassured by those words, but DeeDee couldn't think what else to say. She had to get Elizabeth back in charge, she thought frantically, racing out of the gym and hurrying over to the car she'd borrowed from her mother for the day. There was no way she could take care of all this stuff herself. She'd go positively mad!

"Jess," Elizabeth said anxiously, hurrying into

her bedroom, "you've got to do me an enormous favor. Todd just called me from the talent-show meeting, and he said that DeeDee's on her way over here right now. Will you tell her I can't come downstairs because I've got laryngitis? And that I can't get out of bed for the next couple of days?"

"Have you gone mad?" Jessica said, staring at her twin in disbelief. "You sound perfectly fine to me!"

"It's the only thing we could think of." Elizabeth sighed. "Anyway it isn't my idea; it's Patty Gilbert's. But the plan is to let DeeDee take care of the whole talent show so she'll get her self-confidence back. And I'm supposed to be too sick to—"

"How is messing up the talent show going to help her self-confidence?" Jessica demanded. "OK, OK," she said, seeing the expression on her twin's face as the door bell rang. "Shh," she added, her blue-green eyes twinkling. "You're supposed to be sick!"

Jessica hadn't seen DeeDee since the previous Sunday evening, when she'd told her about Bill and Dana. And she wasn't sure how thrilled the girl would be to see *her*. But DeeDee looked too distraught about the talent show even to register that Jessica was the same person who had engineered the break-up between her and Bill.

"Jess," she gasped, "I've just got to talk to Liz. Is she upstairs?"

"Whoa!" Jessica laughed, opening the front

109

door and gesturing for DeeDee to come inside. "I'm afraid she won't be much use to you in her present condition," she said sadly. "Maybe *I* can help you."

"*What* present condition?" DeeDee demanded. "I *have* to talk to her! Everything's gone wrong, Jess—absolutely everything! The sound system doesn't work, and the lights are broken, and the costumes got messed up, and—"

"Well," Jessica broke in, "*you* can talk to *her*, but I'm afraid *she* can't talk to *you*."

"Why not?" DeeDee demanded.

"Laryngitis." Jessica sighed. "An acute case. Very acute, in fact. Dr. Abrams didn't think there was a lot of hope at first, but now he says if she just stays in bed for *three* days and drinks plenty of fluids and doesn't use her voice one little bit, not even to ask for a glass of water or talk in her sleep or *anything*, she might pull through." Jessica stared at DeeDee to make sure she saw how serious the whole thing was. "We're all *terribly* concerned," she added pointedly.

DeeDee gasped. "What's going to happen to the talent show?"

Jessica pretended to think for a minute. "Well, Liz left a list of instructions here," she said, taking the guest list for her party out of her notebook. "Hmmm. Oh, yes. She's written down that DeeDee should take over for her. And be sure to thank her, it says."

"But I can't take over!" DeeDee shrieked, her

110

face going pale. "Jess, there's no way! It's all fallen completely apart, and I can't—"

"DeeDee," Jess said sweetly, laying a hand on the agitated girl's arm, "you *must* preserve your voice. We can't have *two* directors coming down with laryngitis in the same week, can we?"

Her mouth dropping open, DeeDee stared at Jessica. She wanted to tell Jessica how impossible it was for her to take the whole talent show on at this point, but she couldn't get the words out of her mouth. "Thanks, Jess," she managed weakly at last, turning on her heel and hurrying back to the car.

For the next hour, DeeDee barely stopped to think. She drove back to school in a daze, parking the car in the lot again and hurrying in the back entrance of the school, near the auditorium. "First things first," she muttered grimly. "I've got to see Mrs. Howard about a sewing machine and find someone—somewhere!—who knows something about the lighting system and the microphones. And then . . ."

"DeeDee!" a familiar voice exclaimed. It was Bill, who was standing outside the locker room, talking to Dana Larson.

"Bill!" DeeDee exclaimed, remembering that she hadn't returned his call. "How are you?"

He looked wonderful, she couldn't help noticing. His hair was still wet, combed back the way she loved it. *Used* to love it, she reminded herself.

"I'm OK," he said, giving her a big smile. "But

111

how are *you*? You never called me back last night," he said accusingly.

Breathlessly, DeeDee explained that Elizabeth was sick and she had to take charge of the talent show. "I've never been so busy in my entire life," she gasped, bursting into laughter at the thought of the way the meeting had gone earlier that afternoon. "If this thing is going to take place at all on Sunday, either a miracle's going to have to happen, or—"

"You'll pull it off," Bill said, looking at her admiringly. "You're pretty good in a crisis."

Dana Larson had been listening to this exchange without a word. "Hey, is it too late for The Droids to sign up?" she asked suddenly. "It would be fun to be in a talent show!"

"Sure," DeeDee said, turning to Dana and smiling. "We need all the help we can get." *I can't believe it*, she thought to herself in disbelief. *I'm talking to Dana—and I'm not even jealous!*

Maybe it was because of the way Bill was staring at her, she thought, a blush creeping across her neck and face. It didn't look as though Dana was the one on his mind.

But DeeDee didn't have time to think about Bill right then. She was simply too busy—and whatever he had on his mind, Bill Chase was simply going to have to wait until after Sunday night to talk to her about it.

And that was all there was to it!

112

Eleven

The way Elizabeth saw it, she could hardly go to school on Friday. What was she supposed to do if she saw DeeDee—pretend she'd come to school even though she was supposed to be half-dead from laryngitis?

"Of all the luck," Jessica grumbled. "Why can't *I* come up with fake diseases? I could stay home and pretend to nurse you," she said suddenly, a gleam of inspiration in her eyes.

"Forget it," Elizabeth had told her. "It's bad enough I'm skipping school. You'd better go, Jess."

"Fine," Jessica had said sulkily, slamming the front door behind her.

Elizabeth spent the morning catching up on schoolwork, but she couldn't resist going to the mall for an hour or two after lunch. Actually, she enjoyed herself so much she didn't get home till almost three-thirty. She had taken the bus, since Jessica had the Fiat, and as she neared the

Wakefield house from the bus stop, she was startled to see a police car in the driveway. She hurried up the front walk.

"I am *not* a burglar," Jessica was saying crossly, her arms folded and her eyes flashing fire. She was arguing heatedly with two policemen.

"Jess, what's going on?" Elizabeth demanded.

"Liz!" Jessica cried, her face brightening with relief. "Will you tell them that I'm not a burglar? I live here!" she cried, stamping her foot in frustration.

"Who said you were a burglar?" Elizabeth asked, completely confused.

"My name is Sergeant Malone," the first officer said to Elizabeth, showing her his identification. "Mr. Wakefield left word at the station that they'd be out of town, and we've been keeping an eye on the house. This afternoon we happened to notice someone was trying to climb in the front window."

"I forgot my key," Jessica pointed out, as if that explained everything. "I thought my sister was going to be at home," she told Sergeant Malone, "but"—she turned to glare at Elizabeth—"she was out. So I tried to get in through the window. And then you came along and practically tried to arrest me."

"I think we can let you go this time," Sergeant Malone said, a twinkle in his eye. "It's a little too crowded down at the station house as it is."

"Thanks, Officer," Elizabeth called as the two

men turned and started down the walk toward their car. "For looking after the house, I mean," she added quickly, squirming under Jessica's murderous gaze.

"I thought you were so good at handling things, Jess," Elizabeth said lightly, taking her keys out of her bag. "I mean, if you're capable of having a party and everything with Mom and Dad gone, I should think you could remember a silly little thing like your keys. Right?"

"You, Miss High-and-Mighty Wakefield," Jessica fumed, "are supposed to have laryngitis. Right?"

"Right," Elizabeth said, suddenly bursting into giggles at the thought of Jessica getting caught by the police as she tried to squirm in through a window. "So what?"

"So, shut up!" Jessica snapped, dropping her books in the hallway and racing upstairs to her room.

"Mrs. Abernathy?" DeeDee said. She was in the school office, using the telephone to reach the president of the PTA. "My name is DeeDee Gordon, and I'm in charge of the talent show Sweet Valley High is putting on this Sunday evening."

"Yes?" Mrs. Abernathy said, sounding perplexed.

"Well, I'm afraid there's been a bit of confusion," DeeDee said, twirling the telephone cord around her finger. "We had hoped to use the school auditorium for the talent show, and I understand the PTA is planning to have a meeting there. Is there anything we can do, or is it too late?"

Mrs. Abernathy proved to be much more agreeable than DeeDee could have dreamed. Yes, she *had* heard about the talent show from Winston Egbert's mother. And so many of the PTA parents had children in the talent show it seemed a shame for them not to turn up anyway, and watch the show instead of having a meeting. She even offered to arrange to serve refreshments after the show. "The PTA rarely gets a chance to mingle with the students," she said, chuckling. "I think we'll all have a wonderful time."

DeeDee felt elated. She had convinced Mrs. Howard to lend her a sewing machine until Monday morning, and Olivia was in the home economics department right then, busily finishing the costumes. All DeeDee had left to do was to see about the lighting system. The audio equipment was already being repaired, and Ken and Winston were trying to round up some friends to sell the tickets. Winston had decided he would be an usher until he had to get ready to go on stage for his magic act.

DeeDee was supposed to meet Mr. Jenkins, the electrician the office had called, in five minutes in front of the auditorium. She hurried down the hall, humming to herself, barely able to keep her feet on the ground. It was working! she thought, still unable to believe it. She'd never thought it would all get pulled together in a million years—that *she'd* be able to pull it together. But somehow it was working!

Her mind was so busy churning through the events of the past few days that DeeDee barely noticed where she was going—until she had run straight into Bill, who was coming out of Mr. Fellows's room.

"Whoa!" Bill cried. "Where are you going in such a hurry? Why is it I only see you in fast forward these days?"

"Bill!" DeeDee gasped. "Gosh, I'm sorry," she said, laughing. "I don't know where my mind was. I almost knocked you over!"

"Where are you going?" Bill asked curiously. "I don't suppose you have time for a talk? Or maybe a Coke at the Dairi Burger?"

"Gee, Bill, I'd love to," DeeDee said. "I wish I could. But I've got to go see how things are going in the auditorium."

"How are the sets going?" Bill asked, falling in step behind her. He looked as if he really wanted to know, DeeDee thought happily. As if he still cared.

"Pretty well," she told him, surprised by how confident she sounded. She *felt* confident, she realized with a start. It was as if some bad spell had been broken and she was herself again. "There were too many sets for me to do myself, so I designed them and had other people paint

117

them. Some of the designs I've done are good enough that I've been thinking about going back to those classes," she admitted. "I really miss the formal training."

Bill shook his head. "You sound so different. Gosh, Dee, it's been such a short time, and I feel like so much has happened that I don't know about. When are we going to be able to catch up on things?"

DeeDee shook her head. "I don't know." She sighed. "Everything's so crazy with this talent show. Are you coming to watch it?" she asked shyly, barely daring to hope he'd say yes.

Bill looked delighted. "Of course I am," he said warmly. "Dee, I wouldn't miss it for the world!"

DeeDee felt a lump forming in her throat. Maybe, just maybe . . . she thought.

But she couldn't let herself think about it yet. If things worked out with Bill, they'd work out. In the meantime, she had a show to organize!

"Dee," Patty said, "is there any way I can drag you away from all this to have a cool drink somewhere? I feel like we haven't had a chance to talk in ages."

It was almost five o'clock, and DeeDee was exhausted. Exhausted, but happy. It looked as though the show was finally in good shape. Half of the sets were already standing in the wings, and the rest would be set up the next morning.

The lighting was working, the costumes were prepared—and everything looked pretty good.

"I'd love a break," DeeDee said gratefully. She really relished the chance to see Patty outside of all this chaos, too. It seemed like ages since they'd had a real talk. In fact, DeeDee realized with a start, she'd barely talked to Patty since her fight with Bill. *I wonder why*, she thought. Was she afraid to tell Patty? Afraid of disappointing her?

As if a good friend would be disappointed, she thought, shaking her head. *I must've been nuts!*

Twenty minutes later DeeDee and Patty were sitting outside in the last bit of sunlight at the Box Tree Café, sipping iced tea and exchanging thoughts about the day's meeting.

"I've got to hand it to you, Dee," Patty said, her brown eyes glowing admiringly. "You really managed to get everything together at the last minute. I have to admit, I had my worries there for a while, but it all looks terrific now."

A wave of pleasure rolled over DeeDee.

"There's something else," Patty said in a low voice. "I saw that set you made for my routine today for the first time. Dee, it's gorgeous. I got tears in my eyes when I saw it. You must've worked so hard!"

"I've missed you, Patty," DeeDee said, almost shyly. "I felt like something had come between us—some kind of wall. Maybe I wanted that set to be kind of a token of our new friendship."

Patty swallowed hard, moved. "I felt like

119

something had come between us, too," she admitted. "I wasn't sure what it was or how to fix it. It seemed to me that you had changed, that all that mattered to you was Bill. You talked about *him*, not about you, and that made me feel kind of sorry."

DeeDee shook her head. "I think I was going through a bad time," she said slowly. "I had some misconceptions about the way a relationship should work. The way I saw it, love is threatened by individual achievement—that is, the achievements *I* had. I saw these people around me—my mother, the teacher at my art courses—going through painful divorces. And I was so happy to be with Bill. I didn't want to lose him. So instead, I guess I kind of lost myself."

"How are things with Bill now?" Patty asked gently.

DeeDee sighed, tears welling up in her eyes. "You know, I think about him a lot. I really miss him. I don't want to go overboard the other way—to concentrate so much on myself, on my own activities, that I forget how important it is to love and be loved. I sort of hope we can get back together, but I'm not sure we're ready yet. Maybe we need more time."

Patty nodded thoughtfully. "I should tell you," she said slowly, "that Bill came by to talk to me yesterday. I think he's really upset about what happened. He told me about Dana—"

"Oh," DeeDee broke in, embarrassed, "that was nothing, *honestly*."

Patty smiled. "I don't blame you," she said. "I'm pretty jealous of Jim sometimes. And Bill's worth it! But you know, Dana has a boyfriend. Anyway, what I was going to tell you about Bill is that I think he really wants to get back together with you."

DeeDee was quiet for a minute. She wasn't certain what to say. "I think Bill and I really need to talk," she said at last. "But all I know is this, Patty: If we do get back together, I'm going to have to find a way to balance things better. It's really hard to be close to someone and not get swallowed up. I'm going back to my art classes next week, and I'm going to make sure I stick to them. And I'm thinking of studying a language after school, too. I'd really like to learn German. I just have to remember that however important Bill is, he can't be my whole life. I have to be able to do some things for myself. And I have to be a whole person—not just half of a couple."

"Dee," Patty said, her brown eyes shining, "did I ever tell you that you're the most sensitive, thoughtful, articulate friend I have?"

"Does that mean," DeeDee asked, a twinkle in her eyes, "that you're paying the bill this time?"

Patty groaned, the laughter in her eyes giving away the fact that she wasn't one bit bothered. "OK," she said grudgingly. "But only if you promise that if I ever get to dance on Broadway, you'll do all the sets!"

"It's a deal," DeeDee said, standing up and grabbing her purse.

Linking arms, the two girls headed inside to the cashier, convulsed with laughter for no good reason at all.

Twelve

"Jessica," Caroline Pearce exclaimed, "this party is absolutely fabulous!"

"Thanks," Jessica said airily, surveying the scene around her with private satisfaction. She had moved all the furniture back against the walls in the living room and had turned her father's stereo up all the way. Food was set up on the coffee table, and the people who weren't dancing were standing around in the front hall or the kitchen, drinking soda and sampling the miniature pizzas—perfectly made this time—that Jessica had just taken out of the oven.

So far it looked as though it was going to be a pretty good party, Jessica thought, breathing a sigh of relief. The only thing worrying her was that Lila's friend Drake hadn't shown up—or any of his friends. There were enough guys to go around, but Jessica was expecting a big influx soon from Pi Beta Alpha, the sorority she and Elizabeth were in at school. They would need more guys, she thought anxiously, turning from Caroline to look for Lila.

She spotted her across the room, talking to Peter West. Peter, a senior who had started his own computer consultancy and was supposed to be making a fortune already, was just the sort Lila would be interested in, Jessica thought.

Lila and Peter were arguing about health foods when Jessica approached. "You've got to *feel* it," Lila was saying. "You just have to be so in touch with your body that you *know* what sort of things to put in it."

"Lila," Jessica hissed. "Can I talk to you for a second?"

Lila gave Jessica a look of immense irritation. "I'll be back in a minute, Pete," she said in her most flirtatious way. "Don't go away."

"He'd better not," Jessica muttered, dragging Lila into the kitchen. "Once everyone gets here from Pi Beta Alpha, we're not going to have nearly enough guys. What happened to Drake and all his fraternity brothers? I was counting on at least half a dozen of them, and it's already—"

"Jessica," Lila said complacently, "do you have any idea what time it is?"

"I don't know," Jessica said, nonplussed. "About ten o'clock, I guess. Why?"

"Because," Lila said, as if she were explaining something to a baby, "these are *college* guys, Jess. No one at college ever goes to a party before ten-thirty at the very earliest! They'd rather die. It's *so* uncool to be early."

"Oh," Jessica said weakly, feeling like an idiot. "OK. I guess—"

"Jessica!" Elizabeth called. "Mrs. Beckwith just called. She wants you to turn down the music!"

"Oh, no." Jessica groaned. She had thought one of the neighbors might complain, but she had hoped they'd wait a little longer!

Music was booming from the stereo, but it was impossible for Jessica to make her way through the dense crowd of dancers to turn it down. *I'll get it in a minute*, Jessica vowed, hurrying over to the coffee table to see if any of the platters of food needed refilling.

"Jess!" Lila shrieked over the pounding music. "It's the door bell. I think Drake is finally here!"

Jessica hurried out to the front hall, making a mental note to close the door to her mother's study after she turned the music down. *That's all I need*, she thought. *If someone gets in there and wrecks Mom's plans, I'll never live to see my seventeenth birthday!*

An expectant smile on her face, Jessica opened the door—and felt the skin prickling on the back of her neck.

Jessica Wakefield was scared to death.

She had never seen so many guys in her whole life, all huge, all eighteen or nineteen—or even older—and all reeking of beer. She felt positively sick.

They must have the wrong house, she thought

weakly, wondering if she could get her courage up to shut the door in their faces.

"Lila!" one of the mob bellowed, stumbling into the front hall and engulfing Lila in a huge hug.

"He's Drake," Lila said, then turned to Jessica. "These are Drake's friends, I guess—"

And at that, a dozen enormous, drunken guys came stampeding inside.

"Jessica, we're out of—" Elizabeth stopped dead in her tracks, her mouth dropping open.

"What's going on?" she whispered to her twin, the empty soda bottle in her hand forgotten. Jessica could barely speak. She was watching with disbelief as the mob of college guys crashed into the living room.

"Jess, who *are* those guys?" Elizabeth demanded. "We've got to get them out of here before they trash the whole house! Phew," she said a moment later, her nose wrinkling. "They smell *terrible*, Jessica."

"What am *I* supposed to do?" Jessica demanded, anguished. "Maybe it'll be all right," she said at last. "I'm sure they're all nice guys, or they wouldn't be friends of Drake's."

"Who's Drake?" Elizabeth asked, completely baffled. "And, Jessica, we've got to do something about that music. Mrs. Beckwith is going to have a fit!"

Taking a deep breath, Jessica forced her way back into the living room. Behind her, she heard the door bell ringing again. Elizabeth opened the front door, and all the remaining members of Jessica's sorority spilled into the house, giggling and chattering and slipping out of their jackets.

"There just isn't enough room." Jessica moaned and covered her face with her hands.

Just don't let anything horrible happen, she prayed, afraid to look around the living room and see what was going on. *Please, God, just don't let them completely destroy the house!*

By eleven-thirty the party was in full swing. Most of the food and all of the soda was gone, and to Jessica's dismay the college guys started pulling six-packs of beer out of the trunks of their cars and bringing them inside. A thin, silly senior named Louisa, who was in Pi Beta Alpha, was drinking beer at an alarming pace, and when she wasn't drinking, she was dancing wildly with one of the college guys, who turned out to be named Ted. Drake had pulled Lila down on the couch and begun to kiss her, and after about ten minutes of that, Peter West left in a huff, slamming the front door behind him. Jessica had turned the stereo down four separate times, but someone kept turning it up again. She was fighting a losing battle, she realized at last. She was just going to have to relax and have a good time.

"Jessica!" Elizabeth screamed from upstairs at twenty minutes to twelve. "It's Mrs. Beckwith again, and she's furious. She says if you don't turn the music down, she's going to call the police!"

"Damn," Jessica muttered, pushing her way over to the stereo and trying to make herself heard over the rising din. "We've got to keep this down, you guys, or the police are going to come!"

Nobody listened. Bruce Patman was dancing frenetically with Louisa, who was beginning to look a little green. Drake and Lila were engaged in a heated fight on the couch, calling each other names in increasingly loud voices. Winston Egbert was trying to rehearse his magic act in the corner in front of a fascinated crowd of onlookers, all begging him to turn Mrs. Wakefield's crystal vase into a hard-boiled egg. Jessica was beginning to feel sick to her stomach. She couldn't believe the chaos around her, and all she wanted was to be able to close her eyes and wish them all away. "Why in the world did I ever do this," she muttered, stumbling bleary-eyed into the front hall just in time to see Louisa racing for the bathroom, her hand clapped over her mouth.

Jessica sighed. "What in the world was I thinking of?"

"I'm leaving!" Lila screeched, grabbing her coat and heading for the front door. Drake was staggering after her, a furious expression on his face. "Oh, no you're not," he was shouting.

"Stop it!" Jessica yelled at the top of her lungs.

"Just leave me alone!" Lila hollered at Drake,

jerking the front door open and stopping stock still, her mouth dropping open as she stared up into the deadpan faces of two police officers who were standing there.

"Is this the Wakefield residence?" the first officer said.

"Yes," Jessica said, coming forward, her cheeks flushing as she recognized the police officer who had caught her climbing in the front window after school the previous day.

"You remember me," Sergeant Malone said, unsmiling this time. "And more to the point, *I* remember *you*. Are either of your parents home this evening, or are they still out of town?"

"They're still out of town," Jessica said. "I mean—"

"Is there a person here on the premises over eighteen who claims responsibility for this party?" Sergeant Malone continued, his face grim. "Otherwise, I'm afraid I might have to take you down to the station until I call your parents, Miss Wakefield."

Jessica went white as a sheet. "I—I—"

"I'm over eighteen," a familiar voice said behind Sergeant Malone. The next minute Steven Wakefield stepped out of the shadows. "Jessica, what on earth is going on here?" he demanded, his face turning pale as he caught a glimpse of the chaos inside the house.

"Steven!" Jessica cried. "Thank God you're here!" She had never in her life been so happy to see her brother.

"Have you got some identification on you, son?" the officer asked, his voice softening. Steven obligingly took out his wallet and showed the officer his driver's license.

"OK," Sergeant Malone said, his face still grave, "if this young man is willing to take responsibility and to stay on the premises until the party is over . . ."

"I will," Steven promised. From the way he was looking at her, Jessica had a feeling her ordeal wasn't over yet.

"Then we'll leave it in your hands," the policeman concluded. "But make sure you keep the music down, or we'll be back."

"Thank you, thank you, *thank you*!" Jessica cried, throwing her arms around her brother's neck as the officers closed the front door behind them. "Steve, you saved my life. When did *you* get here?"

"Mom and Dad asked me to drop by if I could to see if you two were all right," Steven said, glaring at her. "I was in the area. I tried to call, but the line was busy. Jess, *what* is going on here?"

"Oh, nothing. Everything's fine," Jessica said, taking a deep breath. "Isn't it, Lila?"

Lila and Drake were still frozen in place, staring from Steven to Jessica.

"Yes," Lila began, "everything's—"

But her voice was cut off by the sound of a crash from the other room.

It sounded like something big and fragile falling to the ground and shattering into a million pieces.

Mom's crystal vase, Jessica thought, standing perfectly still as everyone else rushed into the living room to see what had happened.

Jessica just couldn't bear to move.

She didn't want to know—however horrible it was—she simply didn't want to know.

"I just can't understand it, Jess," Steven said harshly. "I can see why you wanted to have a party, but why did you invite these guys you didn't even know? And why'd you let them bring beer into the house?"

It was almost one in the morning, and half the people had gone home after the disastrous conclusion of Winston's magic act. Winston himself had been almost hysterical after he had broken the vase, and he'd insisted on paying for it, although he admitted he had no idea how he'd get the money.

"Maybe we can all chip in," Olivia Davidson suggested now.

Jessica was barely listening. She was too upset.

She said goodbye to her guests in a complete daze, trying to concentrate on something other than the potato chips ground into the carpet or the cigarette butts in empty glasses.

Finally the last guest was gone, including Lila, who had made up with Drake and left with him—without an apology for the way things had gone. *Lila's probably used to things like this,* Jessica thought sadly. *For one thing, they can afford to have a staff of maids clean up the next day. And they probably throw crystal vases around like Frisbees.*

After Todd said good night, the three of them—Steven, Elizabeth and Jessica—trooped mournfully around the house, surveying the damage. "It's really not *that* bad," Steven said at last, trying to cheer up his sister. "Come on, Jess. We'll get up early tomorrow morning and scrub the whole place. The only real disaster is the vase, and if everyone chips in a few dollars we just *may* be able to help Mom and Dad replace it. So don't—"

"Jess!" Elizabeth wailed. "Come quick!"

"Don't tell me," Jessica said, her aqua eyes filling with tears. "I just can't stand the thought of another disaster."

Elizabeth was standing in the study. "It's Mom's plans," Elizabeth said, her voice quavering. "Jess, did someone get inside the study?"

Jessica clapped her hand to her forehead, her face draining of color. "I knew I forgot something," she whispered. "I meant to close the door. What happened?"

"The Williams plans," Elizabeth said, looking terror-stricken. "Mom had one of the floor plan on her board in here, and someone must've spilled something on it—beer, it smells like," she added, wrinkling her nose.

Jessica couldn't believe it. The one thing her mother had asked her to look out for—the only plan for the firm's most important project of the year—ruined. Completely, entirely ruined!

The beer had soaked through the plan, smudging some of the lines so they were barely visible. Jessica felt as if the whole world had just collapsed around her.

"There's no way we can even begin to fix them," she murmured, tears stinging in her eyes. "Liz, Steve, what am I going to do?"

Jessica stood absolutely still, too miserable even to cry. "This," she said in a barely audible whisper, "is the worst night of my entire life."

Thirteen

Jessica wasn't used to being awake so early on a Sunday morning. And not only awake, but up and dressed and standing on the porch of DeeDee Gordon's house, ringing the door bell and praying someone was home.

After a minute or two, DeeDee opened the door. She was wide awake, looking fresh and happy in a bright-red cotton sweater and a pair of close-fitting blue jeans.

"Hi, Jess," DeeDee said, looking surprised. "What's up?"

DeeDee hadn't been invited to Jessica's party the previous night, and Bill Chase hadn't shown up. DeeDee had no way of knowing the disaster that had befallen Jessica or how desperately she needed help.

"I have to ask you for an enormous favor," Jessica said, coming straight to the point. She couldn't bring herself to try to manipulate DeeDee into helping her. Anyway, this wasn't really *her* idea. It was Elizabeth's. Jessica thought it was worth a try, but she didn't feel very hopeful.

Why would DeeDee do her a favor after the way she'd treated her last week, telling her about Bill and Dana?

"Elizabeth thinks you may be able to help," Jessica said bleakly, stepping inside the Gordons' foyer. "I know I've been a pain to you, DeeDee. And I don't blame you if you say no. But I thought it was worth asking."

"How could I help *you*?" DeeDee asked, startled.

Jessica let out a long, quavering sigh. Step by step she described the events of the previous evening, coming at last to her mother's plans. "They're ruined," Jessica said disconsolately. "Ruined. And it's all my fault."

DeeDee stared at her. "That's awful," she said at last. "I'm really sorry, Jess. But I don't see how—"

"Liz," Jessica broke in, "says that you're a whiz at design. She told me you took a drafting class last year and might be able to help me somehow. She wasn't sure what you could do, but I thought maybe I could just *ask* you."

DeeDee fidgeted for a moment, as if she were trying to think. "How bad is the damage, Jess?" she asked. "You said beer had spilled on the paper, right? But can you still see the original lines?"

"Most of them," Jessica said. "Not all of them—a few got kind of smudged."

"I'll be honest with you, Jessica. I'm not sure I can do anything. For one thing, I've got to get some things ready for the talent show tonight. And more important, I just can't tell if there's anything I can do. If the lines are smudged—"

Color rushed back into Jessica's face. She had to convince DeeDee, she thought wildly. She just had to! Suddenly Jessica was certain that DeeDee could do it, if she'd only agree to come over and take a look at the plans.

"DeeDee," Jessica said, swallowing her pride, "I owe you an apology. A big one. I was furious when Bill chose you over me, and I never liked you much afterward. So when I bumped into Bill at the movies last week, I decided to tell you on purpose, hoping to hurt you. It was a stupid, thoughtless thing to do, but I was still jealous. Anyway, I'm sorry. I deliberately tried to make it sound like some kind of big deal, and for all I know Bill and Dana are just friends."

"They are," DeeDee said gently. "Never mind, Jess. You don't have to apologize just to get me to help you. If I thought there was something I could do—"

"But I really am sorry!" Jessica cried. "I feel rotten. Look, DeeDee, the plans are probably totally ruined anyway. So let's forget about them. I still want you to forgive me. I feel bad, and I'm sorry about the way I behaved."

DeeDee sighed. "Maybe I could come over for

a few minutes," she said slowly, glancing at her watch. "I could just take a look at the plans and see if there's anything—"

"Thank you!" Jessica screeched. "Oh, DeeDee, you're the most wonderful friend in the whole wide world! Thank you *so* much! I promise I'll—"

"That's just it," DeeDee said, reaching in the front hall closet for her jacket. "No promises. The drawing may be far too messy for me to fix. And one drafting class does not a designer make," she added. "I'll do my best, that's all. And my best may just not be enough."

Jessica was overjoyed. She had complete, utter confidence in DeeDee. In fact, she felt like singing for joy as she drove DeeDee back to the Wakefields' house.

DeeDee would be able to fix the plans. She felt sure of it. And they could buy a new vase the next day, and her parents would never know she'd even had a party.

Or so she told herself as she hurried up the front walk with DeeDee—until Elizabeth opened the front door, stared at DeeDee and then at Jessica and announced—all attempts to fake laryngitis forgotten—"Mom and Dad just called. They're at the airport, and they're going to be home in about an hour."

Suddenly Jessica's spirits were like the vase that had hit the floor—shattered into a million tiny bits.

Her only hope left now was DeeDee. But

DeeDee's face was inscrutable as she came inside the house. "Where are the plans?" she asked solemnly. "It sounds like we're in a bit of a hurry, you guys. I'd better get to work right away."

The next thirty minutes were as tense as any Elizabeth and Jessica could remember. DeeDee worked in perfect silence in the study, retracing the plans onto the drafting paper she'd found in Mrs. Wakefield's flat file. She worked carefully and quietly, and the twins sat on the couch watching her in an agony of suspense, dying to ask her how it was going but afraid to interrupt.

At last DeeDee turned to Jessica and gave her a big smile. Right then, Jessica thought with a start, DeeDee looked almost beautiful. "I did it," she said quietly. "It's as good as new. Just throw this thing out," she suggested, crumpling up the original plan, "and tape this copy in place. I think it's pretty good," she added critically, surveying her work. "Anyway, unless she really pores over it, suspecting it's a copy, I don't see how she'd find out."

Jessica threw her arms around DeeDee. "Thank you *so* much," she cried. "Dee, you saved my life," she told her. "I'll be grateful to you for as long as I live."

"Forget it," DeeDee said pleasantly, smiling at Jessica. "I was glad to be able to help. Honest. And I accept your apology," she added, dropping her voice.

The two girls smiled at each other, both relieved that the tension and bitterness between them had evaporated at last.

"Dee," Elizabeth said gently, "*I* owe you an apology, too. I'm afraid I really didn't have anything wrong with my voice. It was a stupid trick—but I wanted you to take over the talent show. I knew you could do a wonderful job, and from what I've heard, you sure have!"

DeeDee turned scarlet. "Boy," she said. "I never would have guessed . . ."

A minute later she began to laugh. "You sure fooled me, Liz. But I'm kind of glad you did. Because you're right—I *did* need to take charge of things. And I think the experience has really helped me a lot."

"Then you're not angry?" Elizabeth asked gratefully.

DeeDee shook her head. "In this case, I think the end really does justify the means," she said slowly. "You had to take an extreme measure because I was really a mess. I needed to be jolted back to reality. And all I can do is thank you."

"*You're* the one who needs thanking," Jessica cried, taping the fresh copy of the floor plan back onto her mother's board. "Dee, if it weren't for you—"

"Hey," Mr. Wakefield called from the front hall, "is anybody home? Where's the welcoming party?"

The twins stared at each other, their aqua eyes widening. Mr. and Mrs. Wakefield were home.

They had made it just in time.

"Girls, how were things around here this past week?" Mrs. Wakefield asked. It was early afternoon, and they had just finished brunch. Mr. Wakefield had told them at length about the case he'd been working on, and Mrs. Wakefield had told them all about the nightlife in Mexico City. "We had a marvelous time," she said. "But what about you? How were things here?"

Elizabeth and Jessica exchanged glances. Steven had gone back to college soon after his parents got home, leaving the twins alone to confess about their party and the broken vase. This was the moment Jessica had been dreading. And she thought she'd never forgive Elizabeth when her sister bounced up from the table, explaining that she had to get ready for the talent show.

"Can we come?" Mr. Wakefield asked. "We made it home just in time to see Jessica getting cut in half in Winston's magic act, right?"

"Speaking of Winston's magic act—" Jessica began.

"That's my cue," Elizabeth said, crossing her fingers at Jessica across the room and hurrying upstairs to get ready.

Jessica cursed her silently and then took a long breath. "You see, I sort of had this party," she began. "And you know that crystal vase of yours, the one you always told us to be careful of when we were dusting so we wouldn't break it? Well . . ."

Jessica sighed. It seemed too cruel to do this to her poor parents. Here they were, all tanned and healthy and rested. How could she tell them that she'd invited people over to bounce their vases on the floor? Still, it had to be done.

"Winston Egbert broke it," Jessica said in a small voice. "I'm terribly sorry. We're going to take up a collection to replace it and everything. He was trying to turn it into an egg."

"Jessica Wakefield," her father bellowed, "sometimes I think your common sense has been turned into—into—"

"An egg?" Jessica asked helpfully.

"That was one of my favorite vases!" Mrs. Wakefield said sharply. "Jess, who told you you could have a party without asking us first?"

"Well, as a matter of fact—"

"We were counting on you two to behave yourselves," her father said angrily. "Did anything else go wrong?" he demanded, looking stern.

"Well," Jessica said, feeling bleak, "there was the washing machine. But we got a man to come repair it. And there was a tiny little fire in the kitchen, but—"

"Don't tell me." Mrs. Wakefield groaned and shook her head. "Is that it? Absolutely everything? I want to know all the bad news at once."

"That's it," Jessica said quickly. *Thanks to DeeDee*, she thought.

"Well," her mother said, winking at Mr. Wakefield, "maybe we can forgive you this time, Jess. Though I really do think you and your friends should replace that vase. What do you think, Ned?"

"I think Jessica's probably punished herself enough," Mr. Wakefield said, grinning. "From what I remember about throwing parties without permission, it's rarely as much fun as it seems. Am I right, Jess?"

"You wouldn't believe how right you are," Jessica said.

And she shook her head in despair, remembering how wretched she had felt that morning.

What a miracle that everything's OK now! she thought. *All I can say is, thank heavens for DeeDee Gordon!*

Fourteen

The lights in the auditorium were dimmed, and Elizabeth felt butterflies in her stomach as she stood up to face the audience. The place was packed. She couldn't believe they had such a good turnout! The stage was all ready, and as Elizabeth stood up, a spotlight settled on her, illuminating her face as she began her opening speech before turning the stage over to Mr. Collins, who would be the MC for the show.

"An event like this one takes an enormous amount of preparation," Elizabeth began, trying to find a familiar face in the audience to fasten on so she would feel less nervous. Catching her parents' gaze, she felt reassured at once, and her voice stopped shaking. "I'm telling you this not to make it seem like *I* did a lot of work, but because I want to single out the person who really made this evening possible."

Elizabeth proceeded to tell the audience how much work DeeDee Gordon had done. "It's hard to conceive of the number of tiny things that can go wrong at the last minute when you're arranging a show like this," Elizabeth concluded. "DeeDee managed the whole thing so beautifully that few of the rest of us realized how close we were to *not* having a talent show.

"Moreover, DeeDee is responsible for designing the wonderful sets you'll see in each of tonight's talented performances," Elizabeth added. "Now I hope you'll sit back and judge Sweet Valley High's talent for yourselves. But first, I hope you'll join me in giving DeeDee Gordon the enormous hand she deserves so much."

Elizabeth sat down, listening to the applause. *I never thought she'd be able to do it,* she thought admiringly. *But she sure showed me!*

"DeeDee! DeeDee!" a group of students started chanting. The cheer caught on. It was obvious no one would be quiet until DeeDee got up to make a speech, too.

The applause when DeeDee made her way up to the podium onstage was deafening. Trying to blink back the tears, DeeDee faced the audience.

"Thank you," she said when the room had quieted. "I'm not really sure what to say, but I'd like to thank everyone who's been involved in the show for being so cooperative. And a special thanks to Liz and Patty, who took the risk of letting me take over." Passing the microphone to Mr. Collins, DeeDee left the stage.

Patty Gilbert was waiting for DeeDee in the

wings when she came off the stage, the applause swelling again. "You were wonderful," Patty said, and she hugged her friend tightly.

"Thanks, Patty," DeeDee whispered. "Your plan may have saved my life, do you know that?"

"Then you're not angry?" Patty asked. "I was afraid you'd be ready to kill me when you found out. I didn't want to trick you, Dee. But I knew you could do it. I just wanted *you* to know it, too."

"I couldn't care less what you and Liz did." DeeDee giggled. "I'm just having such a good time here tonight. And I feel really proud to have been involved in this whole thing."

"I'm going to dance my heart out," Patty told her, squeezing her hand. "Your set's going to give me inspiration."

DeeDee had a feeling she might be right. After all, it had given *her* inspiration, DeeDee thought. After she had finished the set for Patty, she had felt ready to tackle anything. And it was a good thing she had! Because on top of having to organize the talent show, she'd had Mrs. Wakefield's plan to retrace. It had been a long time since DeeDee had had so many people depending on her. And she found she really liked the feeling.

Olivia Davidson was the first entrant in the show. She played a love song on her guitar, and she sang in a sweet, clear voice that made tears come to DeeDee's eyes.

She wondered if Bill was in the audience. The song used to be their favorite. Did he recognize it? Did it still make his heart beat faster?

She didn't have to wait long to get the answer to her question. A moment later a shadowy form was beside her in the wings—blond-haired, strong, gorgeous. It was Bill.

"I watched you leaving the stage," he whispered. "And I came back to say congratulations to you. You've done a great job tonight, Dee."

"Thanks," DeeDee said, her eyes shining.

"Can I kiss you?" Bill whispered huskily, leaning forward in the shadows.

DeeDee nodded, her heart too full to speak.

His mouth was so soft, so warm. Her heart beat faster as his arms slipped around her, pulling her close to him. "Oh, Bill," she murmured, kissing him harder. "I've missed you so much. . . ."

"Remember this song?" Bill asked, his voice breaking.

DeeDee nodded.

"The night I asked you to go with me it was playing on the radio," Bill whispered, his breath warm against her ear. "Remember?"

DeeDee nodded again. "I'll never forget it," she promised him.

"What if I asked you to go with me again?" Bill asked. "Will you, Dee? Will you give me another chance—give *us* another chance?"

DeeDee swallowed hard. She had been dreaming of this moment for days, but she had never quite known what she'd say in response. Part of her wanted nothing more than to throw herself into Bill's arms, saying, "*Yes*, I'll be yours forever." But DeeDee couldn't help feeling wary. She had learned the hard way that there was more involved in romance than kisses and promises. What had carried them through, she believed now, was the deep, underlying friendship she and Bill had forged before they had fallen in love. What she hoped was that they could find their way to a love that had the solid foundation of friendship within it—mutual trust, respect, and admiration.

She would never again forfeit herself for the sake of a boy—not even a terrific guy like Bill, because DeeDee realized now how much she needed a life of her own.

"I want to try," she said softly, looking deep into Bill's blue eyes. "But I'm going to need to take it slowly. Are you willing to be patient with me?"

"DeeDee," Bill said seriously, taking her hand in his, "you're worth being patient for. Will you be patient with me, too?"

But DeeDee didn't need to answer. The look in her eyes told him everything he wanted to know.

Elizabeth was sitting at the back of the auditorium, near the judges' table, laughing as she watched Winston's antics onstage. Jessica looked absolutely ridiculous in the box Winston and Ken had put her in. And the longer they sawed away at it, the more comical the whole skit became.

They're fabulous, Elizabeth thought, wiping the tears from her eyes. Ken was such a good straight man to Winston's clownishness, and Jessica's genuine bewilderment made the whole routine even more hilarious. None of the tricks Winston tried worked, and each time one failed, Jessica looked so crestfallen the whole audience screamed with laughter.

At last the threesome stumbled offstage. Todd was next, Elizabeth thought. She had no idea what his routine was like. He'd kept it a secret from her. But she'd soon find out!

The lights dimmed for several minutes while the crew changed sets, and then Todd came onstage, standing soberly before the podium. Elizabeth was startled by how serious he looked. Maybe it was part of his comedy routine—like Ken's straight-man act, she thought.

But it didn't look that way. Todd looked incredibly sad.

After a minute, he cleared his throat. "I wanted to do a comedy routine tonight, but I just wasn't in the mood. So I hope you'll bear with me while I do a serious reading of a poem I've always loved.

"It's called 'Remember,' and it was written by a woman named Christina Rossetti. It has special meaning for me tonight, and I hope it will have for you, as well."

Elizabeth almost jumped out of her seat. Todd reading a poem? *That* poem? What was going on?

And why did he look so sad?

Taking a deep breath, Todd began to recite. " 'Remember,' " he repeated, "by Christina Rossetti."

"Remember me when I am gone away,
Gone far away into the silent land;
When you can no more hold me by the
   hand,
Nor I half turn to go yet turning stay.
Remember me when no more day by day
You tell me of our future that you planned:
Only remember me: you understand
It will be too late to counsel then, or pray.
Yet if you should forget me for a while
And afterwards remember, do not grieve:
For if the darkness and corruption leave
A vestige of the thoughts that once I had,
Better by far you should forget and smile
Than that you should remember and be
   sad."

Tears shining in his eyes, Todd turned and walked down from the stage, disappearing into the wings.

The audience was stunned. It was such a shock, hearing this plaintive, melancholy poem from the mouth of a boy known for being cheerful and good-humored. Suddenly the mood of the talent show was altered.

Elizabeth, still standing at the back of the auditorium, barely knew what to think. Her throat ached while Todd was reading. It was a sonnet she had always adored, one she had shown him.

But why was he reading it that night? *Why?*

Something's terribly wrong, Elizabeth thought miserably. *And I've got to find out what it is. I just can't stand this a minute longer.*

Taking advantage of the darkness while the crew was changing sets again, she slipped up the side aisle and disappeared into the wings, determined to find Todd and find out what was wrong.

"I just didn't have the heart to tell you before," Todd whispered, tears in his eyes. "I was too much of a coward. Besides, I kept hoping I'd heard wrong, or that my father's company would change their minds."

"Todd, what *is* it?" Elizabeth demanded, grabbing his hand and clenching it as tightly as she could. "You've *got* to tell me. I'll go crazy!"

"Liz, my father's been transferred," Todd said brokenly, staring down at the floor. *"We're moving to Vermont."*

Vermont! For a minute Elizabeth barely registered what Todd had said. Then, the horror of his words began to dawn on her, and she began to tremble all over.

Vermont! It just couldn't be. . . .

"When?" she whispered, fighting for control.

"In a week," Todd whispered back. "Liz, I know it's hard to believe. When I heard my father talking about it at the office, I thought I'd dreamed it. But it's really true. It's been in the works for ages. He just didn't want us to know until it was definite. He doesn't want to go, but the company is making him. And there's no way . . ."

Elizabeth began to cry silently, still trembling like a leaf.

It was impossible. It just couldn't be happening.

The words of the Rossetti poem echoed in her imagination, bringing on a new flood of tears. *"Better by far you should forget and smile . . ."*

But there would be no such thing as forgetting—not Todd. And she had a feeling there would be no such thing as smiling, not ever again.

"Todd!" she cried. And the next minute they were in each other's arms, holding on to each other as if they'd never let go.

Can Elizabeth survive the heartache of losing Todd? Find out in Sweet Valley High #23, **Say Goodbye.**